Hans Koppel is a pseudonym for an established Swedish author who was born in 1964 and lives in Stockholm.

NEVER COMING BACK

HANS KOPPEL
TRANSLATED BY KARI DICKSON

PEGASUS CRIME

NEW YORK LONDON

NEVER COMING BACK

Pegasus Books LLC
80 Broad Street, 5th Floor
New York, NY 10004

Library of Congress Cataloging-in-Publication Data is available.

ISBN: 978-1-60598-391-2

10 9 8 7 6 5 4 3 2 1

Printed in the United States of America
Distributed by W. W. Norton & Company, Inc.
www.pegasusbooks.us

NEVER COMING BACK

1

She'd written that she liked walks in the forest and cosy nights in and was looking for a man with a twinkle in his eye. It was almost a joke, like a parody of the blandest person in the world. She'd also sprinkled her post with smileys. Not a row without a yellow face.

They'd spoken on the phone the night before and agreed to meet at Gondolen.

Anders thought she sounded older than thirty-two. He made a joke about it, said she'd maybe posted a photo that had been taken a few years ago, when she was a few kilos lighter. That was when she sent the most recent one, taken just before going to bed, holding her mobile at arm's length.

Anders looked at it and thought to himself that she could be a hundred and thick as a plank, he couldn't care less.

A drink was best. It usually took about half a minute to decide whether it was worth the effort or not. Dinner was digging your own grave. Sitting there suffering for hours, with a fixed smile. No, anyone with any experience met for a drink. If things went well, you could always go on.

It was half past six on the dot and Anders looked out through the dark to the lights on Skeppsholmen and Djurgården.

What was the flaw, he wondered. It couldn't be the dumb blonde act. Not with that body. Maybe a hideous laugh that pierced your eardrums. Breath like an old dog. Was she frigid?

No, no, keep calm, he persuaded himself.

His mobile started to vibrate. He answered it.

'Hi,' she said. 'It's me. Sorry that I didn't call earlier. I've been sitting in A&E all afternoon.'

'A&E? Are you okay?'

Anders Egerbladh was impressed by his own apparent

2

concern. Now that's what he called being on the ball. A natural enough question to ask, but it would also let him know if whatever had happened would affect his chances of getting into her knickers.

'Fell down the stairs and sprained my foot. I thought I'd broken it, as I could hardly stand on it.'

'Oh, you poor thing . . . '

Anders took a sneaky sip of beer and swallowed it silently so he wouldn't come across as disinterested.

'It's not that bad, really,' she said. 'I've got crutches and a support bandage. But it might be a bit difficult to hobble down to Gondolen, so I thought maybe you could come to my place instead? I've got a bottle of white in the fridge.'

'Sounds perfect,' Anders said. 'I'd love to. If it's not too much trouble, that is . . . We could always meet another time, if you don't feel up to it.'

Jesus, what a genius he was.

'It's no trouble at all,' she assured him. 'I could do with a bit of cheering up after five hours in A&E.'

'Have you had anything to eat?' Anders asked. 'I can pick something up on the way.'

Albert bloody Einstein.

3

'That's sweet of you, but there's no need. My fridge is full.'

She gave him the address and a few quick directions. Anders memorised them and decided to pop down and buy some flowers from the stall. He didn't understand why, but it always worked. Flowers and bubbles.

The rest could wait until next time.

He bought something colourful with long stems and a box of children's plasters from a newsagent. A bit of fun. He thought it would be a smart trick.

With a light step, he headed up to Katarinavägen, turned into Fjällgatan, just like she'd said, walked down the street on the right-hand side until he got to Sista Styverns Trapp, a flight of wooden steps that linked Fjällgatan with Stigbergsgatan above.

Probably named after some drunken docker, Anders mused, who'd spent all his wages before going home to his toothless wife and their fourteen kids who were pulling at her skirt. He didn't pay any attention to the car that was parked by the pavement. He wasn't to know that the woman behind the wheel was the same woman he'd just spoken to on the phone and she was now phoning her husband to say that it was time.

Anders started up the steps between the reverentially renovated old buildings. He imagined himself examining the woman's swollen foot with sensitive hands, his head cocked in sympathy, how he would massage her tight shoulders, be understanding, agree and nod. Had she really had to wait for five hours? The Swedish healthcare system was truly appalling.

Anders didn't know that the photographs he'd seen had been copied from the Internet and were in fact of a single mother from Holland who kept a blog. Nor was he to know that the man he met on the steps had a hammer stuffed up the sleeve of his coat.

They reached the step by the park bench at the same time, each from a different direction. The man stopped.

'Anders?' he said.

Anders looked at him.

'Don't you recognise me?' the man asked. 'Annika's dad. You remember Annika, don't you?'

Suddenly, Anders had a very dry throat. His face, which had been relaxed and full of expectation only moments before, was now wary and stiff.

'After all, it wasn't yesterday,' the man continued, smoothly.

Anders pointed up the steps with his empty hand.

'I'm in a bit of a hurry.'

The man smiled as if he understood and indicated the flowers.

'Meeting someone special?'

Anders nodded.

'And I'm late,' he said, trying to make it sound natural. 'Otherwise I'd love to stop and chat.'

'I understand,' the man said.

He smiled, but made no sign of moving. Anders turned, uncertain, and put his foot on the next step.

'I spoke to Morgan,' the man said as he let the hammer slip down into his glove.

Anders stopped on the step with his back to the man. He didn't move.

'Or rather, it was him who talked to me,' said the man. 'He had a lot to say that he wanted to get off his chest. In the eleventh hour, but still. He was just skin and bones when I saw him. It must have been the morphine that made him get so hung up on the details. He just wouldn't stop talking.'

Anders turned slowly around. On the periphery of his vision he saw something hurtling towards him, but it was too late to duck or raise his arms in defence. The hammer struck his head and broke his skull just above the temple. He was unconscious before he hit the ground.

The man stood over Anders and raised the hammer again. The second and third blows were probably what killed him, but the man continued hitting him to be sure. As if he wanted to erase any impressions and experiences that were stored in Anders' brain, to flatten his entire existence. The man didn't stop until the hammer got caught in the skull bone.

He left it there, glanced hastily around and then walked away from the steps and jumped into the waiting car. The woman pulled out from the pavement.

'Was it difficult?' she asked.

'Not at all,' the man said.

2

Good morning, my name is Gösta Lundin and I'm a professor emeritus of psychiatry and the author of *The Victim and the Perpetrator*, which I presume some of you have read.

No need to put up your hands. But thank you, thank you. I appreciate it.

Before I start, how many of you are policemen? Now you can raise your hands.

Okay, and social workers?

About fifty-fifty. Good, I just like to get an idea. The question is actually irrelevant, as I don't tailor the content of my talks to whichever professional group I'm addressing. I guess I'm just curious. Maybe I would stand with my feet further apart if there were only policemen, sceptical policemen with their arms folded. It's possible, I don't know.

But what does it matter anyway? The theme for today is: How is it possible?

It's a question we often ask ourselves. How is it possible? Why don't they react? Why don't they run away?

Very similar to the questions children ask when they first hear about the Holocaust. How was it possible? Why didn't anyone do anything? Why didn't they escape?

So let's start there. With Adolf Hitler.

As you all know, the moustachioed Austrian is no longer simply a historical figure, he has also taken on mythical proportions. Today Hitler is a yardstick, he is the very symbol of pure evil.

I was just following orders is a stock phrase, and a reminder that we constantly need to question authority and act on our convictions.

Adolf Hitler's polar opposite in this country goes by the name of Astrid Lindgren.

Astrid Lindgren symbolises all that is good in life. The wise and moderate humanist who cultivates and believes in the good in people.

A whole host of edifying stories and phrases have been attributed to Astrid Lindgren. One of the most famous quotes being that sometimes we have to do things even if they are dangerous. Because otherwise we're not human beings, just pieces of dirt.

Adolf and Astrid, black and white, evil and good.

This naive approach to right and wrong is seductive and appeals to us. We want to be one of the good guys, to do the right thing.

Having spent years interviewing both victims and perpetrators – who are also victims, something we often like to forget – I know that the majority here in this room, myself included, could be persuaded one way or the other.

We all have an Adolf and an Astrid inside. It would be foolish to claim otherwise.

But enough philosophising. I'm here to talk about how it works in practice.

The methods used by perpetrators to subjugate their victims are the same the world over and as old as the hills. Bosses use the same techniques as dictators, for the simple reason that there are only two ways of ruling, the carrot or the stick. There might be more of one and less of the other, but all methods are variants of these two.

Unfortunately, I'm not paid to stand here and talk about difficult things in simple language. I'm an academic, after all, and as such have considerable experience in arguing my point and making myself look intelligent and profound.

Which is precisely why PowerPoint presentations were invented.

1. **Removal, social isolation**
2. **Breaking-in violence**
3. **Starvation**
4. **Violence / threat of violence**
5. **Deprecation**
6. **Debt**
7. **Friendliness, privileges**
8. **Denial of the self**
9. **Future with no hope**

Can everyone see? Good. So let's start with the first point . . .

3

Jörgen Petersson waited while the shop assistant rang up a poster of Homer Simpson, a present for his youngest son, whose birthday was coming up soon. Jörgen looked around the shop and a picture by Lasse Åberg caught his eye. For once the motif wasn't Mickey Mouse. The picture was of an old class photo, where half the faces had started to blur and fade. Only a few were still intact. A bit too clear perhaps, but the simplicity of it appealed to Jörgen. He hadn't thought of wasting his days at auctions at Bukowskis in search of suitable work by some overrated ABC artist.

He really didn't understand rich people's fascination

with art. What was it, other than a futile attempt to buy themselves free? A way of distancing themselves from those who had neither the money nor the opportunity.

Jörgen could easily fill the walls of his house with the three masters. Anders Zorn was bearable, but Bruno Liljefors' wildlife paintings and Carl Larsson's happy homes he could do without, thank you very much.

And he already had a Zorn. A poster from the museum in Mora adorned the outside toilet at his cabin. Jörgen looked at it while he was having a shit. Pragmatism and pleasure in gracious harmony. Neither his wife nor his children understood the charm; they would never dream of using the privy when they could sit comfortably indoors with underfloor heating. Jörgen's wife had even suggested they should pull the old thunderbox down.

Jörgen had piped up then, though he normally didn't interfere with decisions made in or about the home. But there were limits. A three-acre property, nearly four hundred metres of beach and he wasn't allowed to have a dump in peace on his own lavvy? In the forgiving company of a half-solved crossword in some bleached old magazine.

It had been a good move on Jörgen's part, to put his foot

down. His wife respected him more as a result and it had consolidated the image of him as eccentric and obstinate, not bad qualities for a rich man.

He studied the Åberg picture for a while and wondered what his own class photos would look like.

Who had he forgotten? Who could he remember?

And who could remember him?

It was possible that they'd read about him. Quite a bit had been written in the financial press and obviously there was a lot of chat about money and progress, but not to the extent that people reacted when he got on the metro.

Jörgen's life was a bit like a successful game of Monopoly. Suddenly there he was with all the hotels and property and the money kept pouring in without any effort. His coffers were overflowing.

He'd made his first million with an Internet company, which, behind all the big words about the future and opportunities, in fact provided run-of-the-mill web design. But that was back in the day when only the initiated understood the concept of IT and the company still had to send its employees on courses to learn how to use the most basic word-processing programmes.

Jörgen had avoided the limelight for the simple reason

that his two colleagues, whom he'd founded the company with, were lens-loving boys.

The company had never run at a profit, but the stock market value nevertheless climbed to over two billion following its flotation. Jörgen had shaken his head at this madness, which annoyed his two ambitious colleagues who let the success go to their heads. They were frequently quoted on the business pages and obviously believed whole-heartedly in their visions of the future. They eventually offered to buy Jörgen out for half the value of his shares and had a good laugh when he accepted their offer, one hundred million kronor in his pocket, thank you very much.

The headline in the paper had read: *Dumbest Deal of the Year?* The greater part of the article was identical to a press release that Jörgen's colleagues had slickly allowed to be sent out.

One year later, Jörgen's former colleagues were in debt, the company had been restructured and was practically worthless.

Then suddenly Jörgen was the one all the papers wanted to talk to. He'd given a firm but friendly no to all requests and sent a silent thanks to his closest friend, Calle Collin, a freelance journalist for the weeklies, who repeated his words of wisdom about living in the public eye whenever he got drunk.

'There's nothing positive about being visible, absolutely nothing. No matter what you do, never show your face. If you're not Simon Spies, keep out the way.'

Calle Collin was one of the few who hadn't been erased from Jörgen's imagined class photo. Who else could he remember? A couple of the pretty girls who had been out of his league. Jörgen wondered where they were today. Wrong, he didn't wonder where they were at all, he wondered what they looked like. He had googled them but hadn't found any pictures, not even on Facebook. Which couldn't just be a coincidence.

He imagined their faces ravaged by cheap wine, consoled himself with the thought that their bodies were in decline. Their tits that had once defied gravity and been the stuff of his wanking fantasies now sagged and spilled out of heavily padded, wired bras.

Ouch, he was sounding bitter. Jörgen was a better person than that.

Or was he?

4

Removal, social isolation

The woman is removed from her familiar surroundings and placed in a new and unknown environment for several reasons. The woman then loses contact with her family and friends, becomes disoriented, geographically confused and dependent on the only person she knows, the perpetrator. This confusion of time and place is amplified by locking the woman up for sustained periods. If her isolation is sufficiently prolonged, the victim is eventually grateful for any form of human contact, even if it is invasive.

'Are you sure? Just one. You'll still be home in time to watch some rubbish on TV.'

'Yes, go on, you don't need to stay long.'

Ylva laughed, grateful for their nagging.

'No,' she said. 'I'm going to be good.'

'You?' Nour scoffed. 'Why start now?'

'Why not? Variety is the spice of life, isn't it?'

'One glass?'

'No.'

'You sure?'

Ylva nodded.

'I'm sure,' she said.

'Okay, okay, it's not like you, but okay.'

'See you Monday.'

'Yep. Say hi to the family.'

Ylva stopped and turned round.

'You make it sound like something bad,' she said, and put her hand on her heart with mock innocence.

Nour shook her head.

'No, we're just jealous.'

Ylva took out her iPod and wandered off down the hill. The wires had got tangled and she had to stop to unravel them before popping the earpieces in and selecting the playlist. Music in her ears, eyes straight ahead – the only way to avoid talk about the weather. There was always some chatterbox who was dying for attention and gossip. The dilemma of small-town living.

And Ylva was an outsider. Mike had grown up here and couldn't take a step without having to give an account of recent events.

Ylva cut down the deserted, picture-postcard lane and passed by a parked car with a tinted rear window. She didn't notice the driver. The volume in her ears was so loud that she didn't hear the car start either.

She only registered it when the car pulled up beside her and didn't drive past. She turned. The window rolled down.

Ylva assumed that it was someone wanting directions. She stopped and wavered between turning the iPod off and taking out the earpieces. She decided on the latter and took a step towards the car, bent down and looked in. A cardboard box and a handbag on the passenger seat. The woman at the wheel smiled at her.

'Ylva?' she said.

A brief second, then that horrible feeling in her stomach.

'I thought it was you,' the driver said, cheerfully.

Ylva returned her smile.

'After all, it wasn't yesterday.'

The driver turned towards a man in the back seat.

'D'you see who it is?'

He leaned forward.

'Hello, Ylva.'

Ylva reached in through the window, shook both their hands.

'What are you doing here?'

'What are we doing? We've just moved here. And you?'

Ylva didn't understand.

'I live here,' she said. 'I've been here for nearly six years now.'

The driver pulled in her chin, as if she found it hard to believe.

'Whereabouts?' she asked.

Ylva looked at her.

'Hittarp,' she replied.

The driver turned to the man in the back seat, astonished, then back to Ylva.

'You can't be serious? Tell me you're not serious. We've just bought a house there. Do you know Sundsliden, the hill that goes down to the water?'

Ylva nodded. 'I live right by it.'

'Right by it?' the woman at the wheel parroted. 'Really? Did you hear that, darling? She lives right by it.'

'I heard,' the man said.

'What a small world,' the woman said. 'Well, then we're neighbours again. What a coincidence. Are you on your way home?'

'Um, yes.'

'Jump in, we can give you a lift.'

'But I . . .'

'Just jump in. The back seat. There's so much rubbish here.'

Ylva hesitated, but didn't have an excuse. She took out the other earpiece, wrapped the wires round the iPod, opened the car door and got in.

The woman pulled out from the pavement.

'Imagine,' the man said, 'that you should live here too. Do you like it?'

'Yes, I'm happy here,' Ylva said. 'The town is smaller, obviously, but the water and the beaches are fantastic. And there's so much sky. Feels like everything is possible. But it's very windy. And the winters are not great.'

'Really? In what way?'

'Wet and bitter. Just sleet and slush, never white.'

'Did you hear that?' the man said to the woman. 'No real winter. Just slush.'

'I heard,' the woman said, and looked at Ylva in the rear-view mirror. 'But then it's lovely right now. Nothing to complain about at this time of year.'

Ylva gave an ingratiating smile and nod.

'It's nice now.'

She tried to sound positive and look natural, but her mind was working overtime. What would the fact that they'd moved here mean to her? How would it affect her life? How much did they know?

The feeling of unease could not be washed away.

'Sounds marvellous, doesn't it, darling,' the man in the back seat said. 'Marvellous.'

'Certainly does,' said the woman at the wheel.

Ylva looked at them. Their responses were repetitive and rehearsed. They sounded false. It could just be the accidental meeting, the uncomfortable situation. She convinced herself that the fear she felt was all in her mind.

'Fancy bumping into you, after all these years,' the man said.

'Yes,' Ylva replied.

He looked at her, studied her without even trying to hide his grin. Ylva was forced to look away.

'Which house is it that you've bought?' she asked, and registered that her right hand touched her face in a nervous gesture. 'Is it the house at the top of the hill, the white one?'

'Yes, that's the one,' the man said, and turned to look ahead.

He looked normal enough. Ylva let her nerves be calmed.

'We were wondering who'd moved in. My husband and I were talking about it just yesterday. We guessed a family with children ...'

Ylva stopped herself.

'It's mainly people with kids who move here,' she explained. 'You've had builders in. Have you completely redone the house?'

'Only the cellar,' the man said.

'Your husband,' the woman looked at Ylva in the rear-view mirror again. 'So you're married?'

It sounded as though she already knew the answer to her question.

'Yes.'

'Children?'

'We've got a daughter. She's seven. Nearly eight.'

'A daughter,' the woman repeated. 'What's she called?'

Ylva hesitated.

'Sanna.'

'Sanna, that's a lovely name,' the woman said.

'Thank you,' Ylva responded.

She looked at the man, he was sitting quietly. She looked at the woman. No one said anything. The situation didn't allow for pauses and Ylva felt forced to fill the silence with words.

'So, what made you move here?'

She wanted it to sound natural. It was an obvious question, but her throat felt dry and her intonation sounded wrong.

'Yes, why did we move here,' the man said. 'Darling, do you remember why we moved here?'

'You got a job at the hospital,' the woman reminded him.

'So I did,' the man said. 'I got a job at the hospital.'

'We thought it would be good to make a fresh start,' the woman explained, and braked for a red light on Tågagatan.

People were waiting at a bus stop about thirty metres away.

'Listen,' Ylva started. 'It's kind of you to offer me a lift, but I think I'll take the bus all the same.'

She undid the seat belt and tried to open the door without success.

'Child lock,' the man told her.

Ylva leaned forward between the seats and put a hand on the woman's shoulder.

'Could you open the door, please? I want to get out. I don't feel very well.'

The man put his hand into the inside pocket of his coat and took out something square, just slightly bigger than his palm.

'Do you know what this is?'

Ylva took her hand off the woman's shoulder and looked.

'Well, come on then,' the man said, 'what does it look like?'

'An electric shaver?' Ylva suggested.

'Yes, it does,' the man replied. 'It looks like an electric shaver, but it's not an electric shaver.'

Ylva tried the door again.

'Open the door, I want—'

The shock made Ylva's body arch. The pain was paralysing and she couldn't even scream. A moment later her body relaxed and she crumpled, her head against the man's thigh. She was surprised that she was still breathing, as nothing else seemed to work.

The man reached over for Ylva's handbag, opened it and poked around for her mobile. He took the battery out and put it in his inner pocket.

Ylva registered the car accelerating past the bus stop. The man kept the stun gun at the ready.

'The paralysis is temporary,' he explained. 'You'll soon be able to move and talk as normal again.'

He gave her a comforting pat.

'Everything will be all right, you'll see. Everything will be all right.'

5

Worth quarter of a billion and what was he doing? Standing in his briefs in the cellar, rummaging through until now unopened boxes, looking for his old school yearbooks. One way of passing the time.

Jörgen Petersson managed to open and go through about half of the boxes before he found what he was looking for. Considering that the treasure was normally hidden in the last chest, he reckoned he'd been lucky.

He flicked through the book, glancing at the class photos, looking for names. Of course, yes. Him. And him. Wasn't she the sister of . . .? The teacher's daughter who looked like she wanted the ground to swallow her up in her picture. The boy who set fire to the playground. The girl who committed suicide. And that poor sod who had to look after his siblings and always slept through the classes.

Madeleine moment after madeleine moment, à la Proust.

Finally, the whole class. Jörgen got a shock. They were just kids, their hairstyles and clothes bore witness to the passing of time. Yet the black-and-white photograph still made him uncomfortable.

He looked at the picture, scanned row after row.

His classmates stared back at him. Jörgen could almost hear the clamour from the corridor: the comments, the shouts, the jostling and laughter. The power struggle, that's all it was. Maintaining your position on the ladder. The girls were self-regulatory, the boys more forceful.

The four loudest at the back. Arms folded and staring confidently straight at the camera, radiating world domination. Judging by their smug faces, they couldn't possibly imagine a reality other than their own.

One of them, Morgan, had died of cancer a year ago. Jörgen wondered whether anyone missed him. He certainly didn't.

He carried on through the rows of names. He'd forgotten

some of them and was forced to look up at the photograph to pull any information from his mental archives. Of course, yes.

But he still didn't recognise two or three of his classmates. The faces and names were not enough. They were erased from his brain, just like the blank faces on Lasse Åberg's picture.

Jörgen looked at himself, squashed into the front row, barely visible and with an expression that was just begging to get out of there.

Calle Collin looked happy. A bit detached, not worried about being an outsider, strong enough in himself.

The teacher, jeez, the old bird was younger in the photo than Jörgen was now.

He put all the removal boxes back and took the yearbook with him up into the house. He was going to look at the photos until they no longer frightened him.

Jörgen went into the kitchen and rang his friend.

'D'you want to go for a beer?'

'Just the one?' Calle Collin asked.

'Two, three. As many as you like,' Jörgen said. 'I've dug out some of our old yearbooks, I'll bring them with me.'

'What the hell for?'

6

Mike Zetterberg picked his daughter up from the after-school club at half past four. She was sitting at a table at the back of the room, engrossed in an old magic box. When she caught sight of her father, her face lit up as it hadn't done since he picked her up when she first started nursery.

'Daddy, come.'

Sanna was sitting with an egg cup in front of her. A three-piece egg cup with a plastic top. Mike realised that her pleasure at seeing him had something to do with him playing captive audience.

'Hey, sweetie.'

He kissed her on the forehead.

'Look,' she said, and lifted the top off the egg cup. 'There's an egg here.'

'I can see that,' Mike said.

'And now I'm going to magic it away.'

'Surely you can't do that?' Mike exclaimed.

'Yes, watch.'

Sanna put the top back on and moved her hand in circles above the egg cup.

'Abracadabra.'

She lifted the top off and the egg had vanished.

'What? How did you do that?'

'Daddy! You know.'

'No, I don't,' Mike said.

'Yes, you do, I've shown you.'

'Have you?'

'It's not a real egg.'

Sanna showed him the middle section that was hollow and hidden inside the top of the egg cup.

'You knew that,' Sanna said.

Mike shook his head.

'If I did, then I've forgotten,' he assured her.

'No, you haven't.'

'Really, it's true. It must be because you're so good at it.'

Sanna had already started to put things back on the plastic tray in the box.

'Do you like magic?' Mike asked.

Sanna shrugged. 'Sometimes.'

She put the colourful lid, which was worn in one corner from frequent use, back on the box.

'Maybe you'd like to get a magic box for your birthday?'

'How far away is that?'

Mike looked at his watch.

'Not in hours,' Sanna said.

'Fifteen days,' Mike told her. 'It says on the clock what day it is.'

'Does it?'

Mike showed her.

'The numbers in the little square tell you what day it is. It's the fifth of May today, and your birthday is on the twentieth. In fifteen days' time.'

Sanna took on board this information without being overly impressed. Watches weren't the status symbol they used to be, Mike thought to himself.

He hadn't been much older than his daughter when he and his parents had moved back to Sweden. They said they were moving home, even though the only home that Mike had ever known was in Fresno, a baking hot town in central California, caught between the Coast Range and the Sierra Nevada. The temperature remained around thirty to forty-five degrees for the greater part of the year. It was too hot to live in, and most people went from air-conditioned houses to air-conditioned cars and drove to air-conditioned schools and workplaces.

Practically no one had a suntan in The Big Sauna, as his parents used to call the place, and Mike got a shock when he came to Helsingborg in summer 1976 and saw all the brown people splashing around in the water, despite the fact that the air was freezing, barely twenty-five degrees.

Mike's parents had spoken Swedish to him since he was little, so he had no problem with the language, except that people often said he spoke like an American. They thought he sounded sweet. Mike had been horrified at having to move back to Sweden and then having the way he talked corrected the whole time.

The children of his own age that he met on the beach the first evening were of a different opinion. They thought he sounded like Columbo and McCloud. And Mike knew instantly that that was no bad thing.

Having noticed the strangely overdressed boy wandering about, the other children had finally approached him and asked if he wanted to play football. Half an hour later, when he'd played up a sweat and peeled off his thick sweater, his new friends discovered his watch, which had no hands, but showed the time in square numbers instead.

Their awe was boundless. The most incredible part about it was that one button had several functions. If you pressed it once, it did one thing, if you pressed it twice, it did something else. Even though it was the same button. No one understood how it worked.

'What do you reckon?' he said to his daughter, thirty years later. 'Are you ready?'

Sanna nodded.

Ylva Zetterberg was conscious.

She lay on the back seat and saw the world pass in the shape of familiar treetops and roofs. She recognised the geography from the movements of the car, knew the whole time where they were.

She was nearly home when the car slowed down to let another car pass and then swung into a gravel drive in front of the newly renovated house. The woman opened the garage door with a remote control, then drove in. She waited until the door had closed behind them before getting out of the car and opening the door to the back seat. Together with her husband, the woman steered Ylva down into the cellar without so much as a word.

The man and woman lay Ylva down on a bed and hand-cuffed her to the frame.

The man then produced a remote control and pointed it at a TV that was mounted just below the ceiling.

'You like watching,' he said, and turned it on.

7

'We have to go to the supermarket and do some shopping,' Mike said.

'Can I sit in the front?'

Sanna looked at him, full of hope.

'Of course,' Mike said.

'Which way shall we go?' he asked, once he'd helped his daughter to belt herself in.

'By the water,' Sanna decided.

'The water,' Mike repeated, and nodded to himself as if to emphasise that it was a wise choice.

He drove down Sundsliden, braking down to second gear

on the steepest part. The water stretched out unashamedly in front of them, almost showing off. It was more open here now than when Mike had been a child, even though there were more houses. As property prices climbed, the view in itself became an asset and the trees were cut down. Snug houses that were built as protection against the wind and weather had been replaced by aquariums designed to display wealth.

'We can go swimming again soon,' Mike commented.

'How warm is it?'

'In the water? I don't know, maybe fifteen or sixteen degrees.'

'You can swim then, can't you?'

'Absolutely,' Mike said, 'but it might be a bit chilly.'

He swung to the left by the house that he'd named Taxi-Johansson's as a child. The owner of the town's only taxi, a black Mercedes with a good many years under its bonnet, had lived in the house and had driven the schoolchildren to the dentist in Kattarp every year. Someone else lived there now and there weren't many who remembered Taxi-Johansson, though there was still an old sign that said TAXI on the garage.

A lot had changed since Mike moved home from the States. Women no longer sunbathed topless and there was a decent variety of TV channels, financed by advertising. Unnecessarily large cars had made an appearance and these days there was no embarrassment in wearing jeans that weren't Levi 501s.

Soon after they'd come back from the US, his mother opened a clothes shop in Kullagatan. Jeans and T-shirts with UCLA and Berkeley on the front. Nearly everyone in Mike's class bought clothes there. His friends got a discount.

The business had been going well and his dad had a job.

As an adult, Mike struggled to remember at what point everything started to go wrong. Sometimes he thought he knew the answer, but as soon as he tried to focus and remember, something else popped up that had been just as decisive.

His father's death was obviously the main cause. He drove into the side of a bridge outside Malmö when Mike was thirteen. His mother always talked about it as though it was an accident, unfortunate and unnecessary.

Mike was seventeen when he realised that it was probably a planned suicide. He'd heard it other places. When he asked his mum, he understood from her rather vague answer that he'd been kept in the dark for four years.

He still remembered the feeling of alienation and emptiness. The utter loneliness. Of having no one. His stomach was empty and there was a metallic taste in his mouth.

'It's impossible to know for sure,' his mum said. 'He didn't leave a letter or anything like that. And he seemed to be so happy.'

According to the experts, that wasn't so unusual. As if a flame flared up and gave the person who had decided to take their own life a brief period of peace.

Mike had long since come to terms with his mother's betrayal, but the knowledge that he was basically alone and couldn't trust anyone was forever branded on his heart.

That sounded a bit stupid, it really did. Nothing had happened to him. And how good were things now? With a wife and daughter and a well-paid job.

And if he was honest, Mike had felt the change long before his father's death. Wrong, it wasn't a change so much as a slide from good to bad.

A couple of years after they'd moved back to Sweden, his dad had lost his job. The jeans shop, which previously had been a lucrative hobby for his mum, became the family's sole source of income. And things started to go downhill when customers chose to go to the shopping centre in Väla instead of buying clothes in town.

It became harder to keep up with the neighbours in a posh part of town where a watch without hands was no longer impressive.

'Can you speak?'

The man slapped Ylva lightly on the cheek.

'Water,' she slurred.

'Makes you thirsty,' the man said.

He'd had the foresight to take a glass of water with him. He held it to Ylva's lips, let her taste it. Some trickled out of the corners of her mouth and Ylva instinctively tried to put her handcuffed hand up to wipe it away.

'You can drink by yourself,' the man said.

He took out a key and undid the handcuff around Ylva's right hand. She pushed herself back against the end of the bed until she was sitting up. She took the glass and drank it down in one go.

'More?' the man asked.

Ylva nodded and held the glass out to him. He went over to the sink and filled it again. There was a kind of kitchen, the sort you get in barracks and building sites and student bedsits. Two built-in hot plates, a sink and draining board, and a fridge-freezer underneath. Ylva thought they were maybe called kitchenettes. She wasn't sure. Nor was she sure why she was thinking about it at all, given the situation she was in.

The man came back, handed her the glass and went over to the TV.

'Why am I here?' Ylva asked.

'I think you know.'

Ylva turned round and tried to pull her left hand out of the handcuff.

'What do you think of the picture?'

The man pointed to the TV screen.

'I don't understand,' Ylva said.

'A bit grainy, but it's on maximum zoom. You might not appreciate it now, but just wait a few days, a week. It'll be different then. I bet you'll be setting your watch by it. Just sitting there, staring, without being able to do anything. But that isn't a problem for you, is it? To just stand by and do nothing, I mean.'

Ylva looked at him, not moving.

'What are you talking about?'

The man struck her across the face with the back of his hand. It was sudden and completely without warning. Ylva's cheek burned, but it was more her surprise at the violence than actual pain that made her gasp.

'Don't play stupid,' the man said. 'We know exactly what happened. Morgan told us. Confessed on his deathbed. In great detail. We'd blamed ourselves until that day. And in fact it was you lot. The whole time, it was you.'

Ylva was shaking. Her eyes were warm and she blinked furiously. Her lower lip trembled.

'Do you think it hasn't haunted me?' she said feebly. 'A day doesn't go by without me—'

'It haunts you?'

The woman had come in through the door.

'It haunts ... *you*?' she repeated as she walked over to the bed and stared down at Ylva, who automatically cowered.

When she eventually looked up, it was with pleading eyes.

'If I could change one thing in my life,' she tried, 'just one ... '

'Morgan only had a few days left,' the man said. 'That made me so angry. That he got away with it so lightly. I suppose you've read about Anders?'

Ylva didn't understand.

'The hammer murder in Fjällgatan,' the man said. 'No? Well, I guess it's easy to exaggerate your own importance when you're part of something. But it got its own tag: "the hammer murder". The papers really went to town on it.'

Mike and Ylva had met at work. Naturally. That was where people usually met, in a sober state and with a function to fulfil. Mike had just started at the pharmaceutical company in Stockholm. Ylva worked in the marketing department and had been asked to interview him for the company's internal magazine.

Neither of them fell head over heels, but they were attracted to each other, and had a good time together. Mike's childhood had been happy compared to Ylva's. Unlike him, she'd never met her biological father, and her mother was a heavy drug user. When she was six, Ylva was placed with foster parents and, following some very stormy years in her teens, she decided to leave home. She hadn't been in touch with them since.

Mike wanted to explore the Stockholm archipelago that his dad had always spoken about with such enthusiasm, so he bought a six-metre sailing boat and they spent the next three summers on it. Mike read the navigation charts. Ylva held the rudder. They had sex in every natural harbour between Furusund and Nynäshamn.

When Ylva got pregnant, they promised each other that, no matter what, things would be just the same as before. Nothing would stop them, certainly not a small child that they could easily take with them.

By the time Sanna was six months old, the boat had been sold and the money invested in a flat.

A year later, Mike was offered a better job in his home town and, to his mother's delight, moved down to Skåne with his family.

Having a small child meant change, a significant transition to a new phase in life. From public transport to a car, from evenings out to dinners with friends, from a mattress on the floor to a double bed and no time to lie in it. The porn films that they'd enjoyed so much were cleared out after Ylva, half asleep, had helped Sanna, then three, to put in a DVD and instead of Gummi Bear cartoons, they ended up in the middle of a blow job.

Ylva had lurched forward and turned off the TV.

'What was that?' she'd asked, embarrassed.

'Ice-cream!' Sanna suggested, an obvious association.

It was another life, very different from the summers on the sailing boat. But it was a good life.

8

'No, no, no, it's Morgan who's dead,' Jörgen Petersson said. 'I remember because I was ashamed of how glad I felt when I read the notice. Cancer of the pancreas, dead within a couple of months.'

Calle Collin nodded.

'Quite possibly,' he said, 'but Anders is dead now, as well.'

'How did he die?'

'He was murdered.'

'Cool.'

'No, I'm serious. The hammer murder up at Fjällgatan. The papers were full of it. That was Anders.'

'The hammer murder?' Jörgen repeated, while he searched his memory in vain.

Calle nodded.

'Never heard about it,' Jörgen said. 'When did it happen?'

'About six months ago.'

'You mean murdered, as in killed on purpose?'

'Yes.'

'Who by?'

Calle shrugged. 'Don't think it's been solved.'

'Why didn't you say anything?'

'I didn't know it was him until a few days ago.'

'Was it a fight or something like that?'

'No idea.'

Jörgen was silent for a moment. 'Jesus.'

'Exactly.'

Jörgen let out a long breath. 'I can't say that I'm sorry.'

Calle turned his face away and held a hand up to his friend. 'That's pushing it.'

Jörgen took a drink of beer and then put the glass down.

'Maybe,' he said. 'But you've got to admit, it couldn't have happened to a bigger bastard.'

'You don't know that,' Calle said. 'People change.'

'Do they?'

Calle didn't answer. Jörgen looked at the class photograph, nodded to himself.

'Morgan and Anders, dead,' he said. 'Then there's only Johan and Ylva left. The Gang of Four reduced to a dynamic duo.'

'The Gang of Four?' Calle snorted. 'Johan lives in Africa,' he continued.

'Africa?' Jörgen exclaimed. 'What's he doing there?'

'What the fuck do I know? What do Westerners do in the Third World? No doubt he's wandering around in weird clothes and half-cut most of the time.'

'Sounds just like the archipelago,' Jörgen said. 'What does he do?'

Calle leaned back in his chair.

'How should I know? I haven't seen him in twenty years. What's with the obsession? Do you really go around thinking about them? Your old tormentors.'

Jörgen didn't look happy.

'When I opened the yearbook it was like going back in time,' he said.

'You wanted to wave your bank book under their noses?'

'At least a balance statement from the cashpoint. I thought

I might just happen to stand in front of them in the queue and leave my receipt in the machine. What d'you reckon?'

Calle Collin shook his head and smiled.

'Do you understand the extent of your illness?'

'Everyone else is invited to class parties and reunions all the time, but not us,' Jörgen said.

'And I'm bloody grateful for it,' Calle retorted. 'And you should be too. Didn't you see that film, *The Reunion*? The same shit over and over again, everyone reverts back to their old roles. It doesn't matter whether you've done time or earned your first billion.'

'I thought it was done automatically with some kind of database,' Jörgen said, in a distant voice.

'What?' Calle asked, without any real interest.

'The invitations,' Jörgen replied, 'to class reunions.'

Calle sighed loudly, finished his beer and pointed at Jörgen's half-full glass. He nodded. Calle got up and went to the bar. Jörgen pulled the yearbook over and studied the class photo again. They were so young in the picture. But he still wanted to hold them to account, each of them, for all the shit they'd put him through. In Jörgen's eyes, there was no time limit. Even though there were plenty who'd had it worse.

Calle put the two beers on the table and sat down.

'You're completely fixated,' he said. 'Why?'

'I don't know.'

'Haven't you got more important things to think about?'

Jörgen shrugged. 'It's not that, it's just . . . '

'Just what?'

'I don't know. It would just be so cool to know what's happened to them all.'

'Because you're a big cheese now?' Calle said.

'No, not at all.'

Jörgen pretended to be insulted. Calle sent him a cynical look.

'Well, maybe,' Jörgen said, eventually. 'But is that so strange? Look at me.' He tapped the yearbook with his finger. 'I don't exist.'

Calle scrutinised his friend for a long time. He didn't smile.

'What?' Jörgen asked.

'I don't think it's very nice.'

'What?'

'What you're doing,' Calle said. 'Look at me: unmarried, no children, a reporter for a weekly. I do saccharine interviews with washed-up TV celebrities and village eccentrics, write racy short stories about young women at their peak, twenty-seven years old. Short stories that are read by women who are seventy-two. Same numbers, just inverted. I have no ambitions, no prospects. My only luxury in life is ice-cream in summer, a beer in the pub and sometimes, when the urge takes me, a trip to the cinema in the middle of the week.'

'And you're complaining?' Jörgen said.

9

Breaking-in violence

Nearly all women who are forced into prostitution give evidence of breaking-in violence and rape by their pimp. Violence is used to establish a clear power structure, and the perpetrator effectively breaks down the victim's initial resistance. Anyone who has been subjected to violence or threats of violence knows what the long-term psychological consequences of this are. Violence is the clearest expression of power.

The woman released the handcuff that kept Ylva's left hand locked to the head of the bed. Ylva massaged her wrist and pulled up her knees.

The man and the woman stood on either side of the bed. Ylva didn't know who to look at.

'Listen,' she tried, 'we need to . . .'

The woman leaned forward with feigned interest.

'Need to what?'

'Talk,' Ylva said, and turned to the man with pleading eyes.

He had his hand down his trousers. What was he doing?

Ylva looked at the woman, who was smiling at her.

'Yes, talk, certainly. You can talk and we can listen. Sit here and listen to what you've got to say, try to understand. That's certainly one way of doing it.'

The man played with his penis, got an erection.

'Give me your hands,' the woman said to Ylva.

The man undid his trousers and stepped out of them, pulled down his pants. His hard-on was visible under his shirt.

'Your hands,' the woman repeated.

Ylva threw herself off the bed, in the direction of the locked door. The man quickly caught up with her. He grabbed hold of her arm, spun her round and hit her across the cheek again with his open hand. He twisted her arm up behind her back and pushed her in front of him over to the bed.

Ylva kicked and screamed, which only seemed to make the couple more determined. The woman pulled Ylva's jeans down to her knees. The man shoved her across the bed. The woman went round to the other side and yanked Ylva's head up by the hair.

'I didn't do anything,' Ylva cried.

'No,' the woman said. 'You didn't.'

Just then, Ylva felt the man force himself into her.

Her eyes smarted with the pain and her vision blurred. But still she could see the woman smiling at her.

'When's Mummy coming home?'

'I don't know, sweetheart. She said she might go out with some people from work.'

'Again?'

'She didn't know for sure.'

'She's always out.'

'No, sweetheart, she's not.'

'Always, all the time,' Sanna said, and flounced off to the sitting room and the TV.

She stopped in the doorway and turned round.

'What's for supper?'

'Spaghetti and mince.'

'Red?'

'Red.'

For some unknown reason, their daughter preferred the cheat's version with ready-made tomato sauce to Ylva's far tastier variant.

When it was served later, Sanna would be obliged to pick out with surgical precision any life-threatening traces of onion and red pepper before she could eat. Other than that, she showed remarkable interest in whatever was put on the table. If there was any cause for complaint, it was the time it took for her to eat. A Tibetan monk couldn't have been less concerned about time.

Mike gazed out at the street and wondered if he should give Ylva a quick call, after all. Find out if she was going to come home for supper. He decided not to. For tactical reasons. It wasn't because he was proud.

A year ago, Ylva had had an affair with one of her clients. A restaurant owner with no notable qualities other than a cheesy grin that Ylva couldn't seem to get enough of.

Mike had kicked up a storm. It was a soap opera from start to finish, or at least reminiscent of an episode from one.

Mike was totally dependent on his wife and would rather that she was unfaithful to him for the rest of his life than be forced to live without her.

And yet, in weaker moments, hate was his companion, it latched on to him and walked beside him, too close, constantly tapping on his shoulder, demanding attention and energy.

Do something, the voice insisted. Do something.

In those moments, the world shrunk. The skies pushed down and hovered right above Mike's head, like a basement ceiling.

He'd read somewhere that the person who was unfaithful often felt even worse. That it was all about confirmation and projected self-loathing, all that psychology bullshit that only they believed in and used to justify their behaviour.

Mike enjoyed playing the victim, to a certain extent. Not in the sense that he wanted everyone to know he was a cuckold, but in the privacy of his own home there'd be plenty of self-pity and accusing looks.

In the end, he went too far and Ylva gave him an ultimatum.

'Things are the way they are. Either we put it behind us and move on . . .'

She was standing at the sink peeling potatoes when she said it. She paused, turned around with the peeler in one hand and a half-peeled potato in the other.

'Or we'll need to find another solution.'

Mike had never mentioned the lover's name again.

The woman pulled Ylva's hair hard and forced her face up.

'How does she feel?' she asked her husband.

She didn't raise her voice even though Ylva was screaming and crying and talking incoherently about what had happened.

The woman didn't want to miss a second of her humiliation, the long-anticipated retribution.

'Like putting your cock in a bucket of hot water? She must be wide, she's had that many in there.'

The woman pulled at her hair.

'Well, are you? Wide?'

Ylva was crying and the snot ran from her nose. Her head bounced in time with the man's thrusts. Her face was twisted with pain.

'I think she likes it,' the woman said. 'She seems to like it. You'll have to do it again, darling.'

Ylva pleaded with them.

'Please.'

The woman leaned towards her.

'I won't do a thing,' she whispered. 'I'll just watch.'

The movements quickened and then finally stopped. The man straightened up, out of breath, pulled on his pants and did up his trousers.

The woman let go of Ylva's hair and straightened up as well. She walked in front of her husband and unlocked the door. She let her husband through and then followed.

'You can be grateful there's only one,' she said, and closed the door.

10

Mike cooked the spaghetti and made the red mince sauce. The sophisticated recipe entailed browning the mince, adding Barilla tomato sauce and stirring. The food was served with ketchup and parmesan. Sanna had a Coke as it was Friday and Mike had a glass of red wine, because he felt like it.

'How was school today?'

'Okay.'

'What did you do?'

'Don't know, all sorts.'

Sanna put some food in her mouth.

'But you like school, don't you?'

Sanna nodded as she chewed, mindful of keeping her mouth closed.

'That's good,' Mike said. 'You'd tell us if you weren't happy, wouldn't you?'

He immediately regretted it. It was a stupid question, leading. Excessive anxiety on the part of the parents that could end up as a self-fulfilling prophecy. Fortunately, Sanna's thoughts were elsewhere. For once, she was eating quickly and shuffling her bottom restlessly around on the chair.

'Finished,' she announced and stood up.

She put her plate by the sink and went back to her film.

Mike cleared up in the kitchen and was struck by the guilt of TV parents. He went into the sitting room and sat down beside his daughter on the sofa. It was a cartoon DVD that they'd bought. Sanna had seen the film a hundred times before and knew it off by heart. For some reason, she liked watching films she'd already seen. As if her greatest pleasure was knowing what was going to happen.

'This is a good bit,' she said in advance and leaned in to Mike.

And then she laughed at something funny she knew was

coming up. Mike smiled at the luxury of being able to sit beside his daughter and watch an idiotic film that would otherwise simply pass him by.

'Shall we play a game?' Sanna asked, as the credits rolled.

'Absolutely.'

Sanna went and got a pile of spin-off products from various blockbusters. The rules were difficult to understand and the entertainment value zero.

'Can we build a tower instead?'

'You always want to build towers.'

'I like towers.'

'Oh, okay.'

Sanna sighed as she went over to the play boxes and came back with a plastic tray full of building blocks in various shapes and sizes.

The point was to build the tower as high as possible. They each put on one block at a time, and the one who made it topple was the loser. Mike was careful to lose convincingly. He had no time for parents who competed with their children.

He had discussed this with some colleagues. One of them refused to let his children win. And it was the right thing to do, his colleague argued, because one of his sons had just recently been selected for the junior national handball team.

Mike didn't understand his reasoning. With the best will in the world, he couldn't see the point in playing handball for the national junior team.

He and Sanna made towers from building blocks until it was time for bed.

'When's Mummy coming home?' Sanna asked, as she settled down under the duvet.

'She'll be here soon,' Mike said.

'How soon?'

'Very soon.'

'I want to stay up until she comes.'

'No go, I'm afraid.'

'Why not?'

'Because I don't know exactly when she's going to come home. But by the time you wake up first thing tomorrow morning, she'll be in her bed, I promise. And you'll have to be a little bit quiet, won't you, as Mummy will be tired.'

Ylva was still lying on the bed. She couldn't get up. Only a couple of hours ago she'd wished her colleagues a good weekend and walked down the hill to catch the bus home.

The man and the woman had been waiting for her, offered her a lift. Ylva couldn't say no. You couldn't really, could you, when new neighbours who've just moved in offer you a lift.

Everything had been planned, the rape as well. The cellar room she was in had been built especially for her.

Ylva was only a hundred metres from her own house, where her husband and daughter were waiting for her to come home.

Or maybe they weren't. Ylva had mentioned that she might go out for a glass of wine with her colleagues after work. Would Mike dare to call? Probably not. He wouldn't want to seem weak. When would he realise that something was wrong?

Ylva rolled over on to her side, with some difficulty. Her body was sore and it hurt to move. It took all her energy just to try. She lay there, gasping for breath.

The TV was on.

It was dark outside, the streetlamps glowed in a kind of white halo that made the rest of the picture dark and grey. It was difficult to see the silhouette of their house. But Ylva saw that the light in Sanna's room was still on.

How long would it be before Mike called the police?

Would they let her go before then? They couldn't keep her here.

Could they?

The thought was too much to take in. Of course she would report him. Ylva would report both of them. What had happened twenty years ago didn't really matter.

Couldn't they understand that what had happened had tormented her too? Not in the same way, obviously. But that didn't make it any easier. In a way, it made it worse. They didn't have the guilt, never needed to think about what they could've done.

A day hadn't passed when Ylva hadn't blamed herself. She had gone through all the stages of denial and self-loathing, without finding peace. Ylva would just have to live with it.

She manoeuvred herself off the bed, staggered over to the door on shaky legs, pushed down the door handle and pulled. It was locked. There was a peephole in the door. Ylva tried to look through it, but realised it was fitted the other way round. So that they could look in from outside.

She kicked the door but just hurt her foot and so started to hit it with the flats of her hands in the hope that the sound might be audible on the other side. She stopped to listen for footsteps, but only heard her own sobs. She ended up banging on the door hysterically and screaming as loud as she could.

Ylva didn't know how long she did this for, but when she finally turned her back to the door and sunk to the floor, she had no feeling left in her hands.

She cried and cried, but eventually lifted her eyes and discovered that the cellar room she was in was done out like a studio apartment.

She put her hands flat on the floor and got up with great difficulty. She went over to the kitchenette and opened the fridge. It was empty, except for a half-tube of Primula.

There was a door in the wall opposite the kitchenette. Ylva opened it. A bathroom with a toilet, shower and sink. No window, just a fan, high up on the wall.

Ylva closed the door and looked around. The walls were plastered breeze blocks. The room was twenty square metres, max, just a small corner of the cellar.

Ylva remembered all the pallets of building materials that had been left outside the house, waiting for the new owners. The Poles, who spoke very little Swedish, had tried to answer the questions from inquisitive neighbours.

The cellar. They were going to do something in the cellar. Build a music studio, they thought.

When he'd finished the story, Sanna lay there and traced the pattern on the wallpaper with her finger, as she usually did. She'd asked again when Mummy was coming home and Mike had felt almost guilty.

'Am I not good enough?'

He said it as a joke, but underlying the words was a hurt.

'Mummy will be back soon. She just went out with some friends for a while. Grown-ups have to be allowed to play with their friends too, sometimes.'

Mike thought he sounded false when he said that, but Sanna didn't seem to react.

Fifteen minutes later, he woke up and saw that she was asleep. He hoped that she'd fallen asleep before him, but had his doubts. Carefully, he raised himself up on one elbow. The bedsprings creaked and groaned under his weight but Sanna slept on.

Mike left the bedroom door open. He recalled the feeling of horror when he'd woken up in total darkness as a child with no idea where he was. He didn't want Sanna to have to go through the same thing.

He went down to the kitchen, opened the fridge and looked at the contents without finding anything tempting. He went through the cupboards and was happy to discover a half-full bag of peanuts behind the cereal. He decided that he deserved them, as a brave and currently-as-good-as-single parent, and poured himself a whisky to go with them.

Mike took the nuts and whisky into the sitting room, switched on the TV and watched the end of a film he'd already seen. It was better than he remembered and gave him an inkling of why his daughter always wanted to watch the same film.

When the film had finished, he flicked through the channels without finding anything else to watch. He turned the TV off. There were no curtains in the sitting room and the blue glow of a television at this time of night might be misconstrued.

He went to get his mobile phone. No missed calls or apologetic texts.

It wasn't fair that she hadn't been in touch. After all, it hadn't been definite that she was going out for the evening. She should have phoned to say whether she was coming home for supper or not.

In the end, Mike decided to give her a ring. Officially to make sure that everything was okay and to insist she got a taxi home. Simple concern, he convinced himself, nothing more. He wasn't calling because he was in any way worried that she might be fluttering her eyelashes at someone, or chewing her lip in that deliberately provocative way.

Mike repeated to himself exactly what he was going to say before he picked up the phone.

Just a bit worried. Thought you might call to say whether you were coming home for supper or not. No, no, she's fast asleep. We had a nice evening, building towers. No trouble at all. I'm off to bed now. Can you try to be a bit quiet when you come in, and I'll get up early in the morning and pop down to the shop for some fresh rolls. Have fun. And don't forget to take a taxi home.

But instead of extended ringing and then finally his wife's voice, with a wall of loud music, laughter and happy shouts in the background, it went straight to voicemail. An automated voice told him which number he'd called and Mike pulled himself together.

'Hi, it's me,' he said. 'Your husband. Just thought I'd see how you're getting on. I assume you're out with people from work. Anyway, I'm off to bed now. Take a taxi home, please.

I've had a drink and can't drive. Sanna's in bed. Big hug.'

He hung up and immediately regretted leaving the message. It didn't sound natural, and saying 'your husband' sounded insecure, as if he was nervous and having a go at her, in a don't-do-anything-stupid sort of way.

He sat there and stared at the display on his mobile phone. The screen image was of Sanna and Ylva on the swimming dock at Hamnplan, dripping with water, smiling happily at the camera with the Danish coastline in the background.

Hi, it's me. Your husband . . .

11

Ylva heaved and gasped, tried to think straight. They had driven into the garage, carried her down some steps that swung ninety degrees to the right, west towards the water. They had walked along a corridor, two to three metres long and opened double doors into the room she was in now.

She compared this with her mental image of the house. She'd never been inside before, just seen it from the outside, but she knew that the ground plan was basically square.

Ylva realised that they'd built the room she was in more or less in the middle of the cellar, as far from the outer walls as possible. The breeze blocks that separated her from the rest of the cellar were more than a hundred centimetres thick. They may have insulated the walls even more behind the blocks.

They had built a music studio, a soundproof room where you could make as much noise as you liked without anything being heard outside. So basically, no matter how much she screamed, no one would hear her.

But the room couldn't be completely sealed. There had to be an opening, some kind of ventilation. Oxygen could of course get in through the cracks and joins in the doors and walls, but an extractor would be bigger.

She quickly crossed the room again, opened the cupboard doors, inspected the walls and ceiling, got down on her knees and looked under the bed.

There was a vent in the bathroom and in one of the corners of the room. Ylva took the chair from beside the bed and pulled it into position. She got up on it and put her mouth to the vent and shouted for help. Stretching at such an awkward angle gave her cramp in the neck and she found it hard to keep her balance. She almost fell off the chair a couple of times, but managed to stay upright by bending her knees. She screamed for help, desperate and scared.

She had no idea how much time had passed when she

finally gave up in tears, climbed down from the chair and collapsed on the bed. She looked at the TV screen. The white halos around the street lamps were bigger and the lights in her own house had been turned off. It was night.

Ylva wondered whether Mike had tried to call her. She couldn't be sure. Maybe he'd wanted to, but hadn't dared. Mike was scared that she'd get irritated, that she'd think he was keeping an eye on her, clipping her wings. How many times had she not checked her breath when she felt that he was following her around? Ingratiating and happy to help, but also anxious and on guard.

And even though she'd never said it aloud, the sentence hung in the air and spoke volumes.

You can't lock me up, Mike. It won't work.

Mike dropped off to sleep quickly but woke up again just after two. He saw that Ylva wasn't home yet, went to the loo and then came back to bed. He hadn't bothered to turn on the light in the bathroom and sat down on the toilet for a piss, everything to increase his chances of going back to sleep, but as soon as he was under the covers again, he was wide awake. Red wine usually had that effect. It made him dozy and sleepy at first, but then he woke up with his heart going like the clappers. His brain immediately engaged and proceeded to take him on a twisting and shuddering big dipper ride. The associations were inevitably negative and dark.

Wherever Ylva was now. He could picture it. Her falling back on to a bed, quickly followed by an intent lover who kissed her passionately on the mouth and then on down her neck. The shirt being ripped off, wild, almost like a parody of a film, but to them, natural and real.

Ylva's lover's eager hands drawn to her cunt, her gasps and half-strangled cry as he penetrated.

Mike opened his eyes to clear the images in his head, replace them with what his eyes could see: the window, the clock-radio, his clothes on the chair, the wardrobe and the mirror. Everything was real and existed in the real world.

He turned on the bedside lamp, let his eyes adjust to the light. Time, 02.31. It wasn't that late. Not really.

Ylva had gone out with her colleagues. They were drinking wine and talking loudly about work, male colleagues who for some reason were senior to them and smug with it, about promotions and being overlooked. Or they were telling stories about their husbands. What was good and bad about them. Those who had problems were offered comfort and advice and, when they'd analysed it thoroughly, they raised their glasses and came out with over-confident claims.

I'm absolutely certain . . .

And whatever might follow a lead-in like that.

No, it was men who were absolutely certain. Men without voices. Men in old men's bars, with a cheap pint in front of them. The female equivalent was probably: *Well, I still think that . . .*

Ylva and her female colleagues would soon return to their lives with a lighter heart, having offloaded their problems through the course of the evening.

Mike wondered if he was ever discussed in his role as manager. And if so, what his staff actually said. That he was weak? Probably not, not at work. Vague? No. What negative opinions would they have? Mike reckoned cold, that he was like a robot. They might even call him a psychopath and say that he showed absolutely no empathy. Which was presumably wrong, Mike guessed, because a psychopath was in fact sensitive to signals around him or her and careful to exploit them. Even if he or she decided in the end to ignore them and do whatever was necessary to get their own way.

Mike pushed the thought from his mind, felt almost hot

and bothered by the interest he imagined his employees had in his life.

He fell asleep again, secure in the knowledge that he earned nearly four times as much as Ylva and the life they lived would not be possible without his income.

12

The Gang of Four, Calle Collin thought to himself, and sighed loudly.

Jörgen Petersson had too much money, that was obvious. Too much money, too much time and too little to do. Was Ylva the equivalent of Mao's old widow, was that what he imagined?

Calle almost got annoyed. Why did all the nutters come to him? He was like a magnet for idiots. Did he have a neon sign saying 'tolerant' above his head? Was he too nice? Did they think that because he was a homosexual he understood the pain of being an outsider and so welcomed every man and his dog with open arms?

Probably the latter. Positive prejudice could be just as hard to deal with as negative. Jörgen had called him a good-natured poof. And Calle had asked what that made him, a fag hag?

The Gang of Four. How stupid was that?

What was Jörgen thinking, anyway?

Calle was still lying in bed. He had a headache and was too tired to masturbate. But he could feel the restlessness of the alcohol that was in the process of leaving his body. He had a wank all the same. To blanket his hangover and anxiety and change his frame of mind. He came on his stomach and got out of bed with his hand over the sperm, so it wouldn't drip on the floor. He hurried out into the bathroom, wiped his belly clean, had a piss and went back to bed.

The Gang of Four. As if they were a group of nonconformists in monk cowls who spoke in tongues and were blood brothers.

They weren't that bad. And, anyway, the group kind of disintegrated halfway through Class Nine and formed new alliances and constellations.

Typical of Jörgen to give them a name. The Gang of Four.

He had always overdramatised things as a child. But maybe that was the secret behind his success, that he was not blinded by detail, that he could still see the woods despite the trees.

That was the last thought that went through Calle's head before he happily fell asleep.

13

'Where's Mummy?'

Mike opened his eyes and blinked furiously. Sanna was standing by the bed in her pyjamas. He turned over and saw that Ylva's side of the bed was empty and untouched. No one had slept there.

'I don't know, sweetie. What time is it?'

He reached over for his watch.

'Eight zero seven,' Sanna read on the radio-clock and jumped up on to the bed. 'Has Mummy not come home?'

'I don't know, doesn't look like it. Maybe she stayed over

with one of her friends. Maybe it was late and she couldn't get a taxi.'

'Aren't you going to ring her?'

'Not quite yet. If they were late last night, she'll still be asleep.'

'What if she's not sleeping?'

Which was precisely what Mike was trying to avoid thinking, but his brain didn't care about him, and images rolled in front of his eyes: Ylva dressed in yesterday's party clothes walking from the bus stop, possibly barefoot, holding her heels in her hands. She stops in front of the door, looks down kind of ashamed for a second before plucking up the courage and saying: *Mike, we have to talk.*

That's how he envisaged it, even though she hadn't been wearing high heels or a sexy dress.

Mike sat up.

'She'll be asleep. Are you hungry?'

Sanna nodded with big, exaggerated movements as she leapt out of bed.

'Sugar puffs!'

'Okay, sugar puffs. But you have to eat some bread too.'

Mike put on the coffee and went to get the paper, doing all the things that might be expected of a man who wasn't terrified by the thought that his wife might have left him. He phoned her repeatedly. Her mobile was switched off and went straight to voicemail. Mike left a message.

'Where are you? I'm starting to get worried. Sanna too. Please call us.'

The second time: 'Why the hell is your mobile turned off? That's such a shitty thing to do. Not that I give a damn where you are.'

Breakfast, reading the paper, checking the evening papers online, nothing fast-forwarded the time to nine o'clock, when Mike could reasonably phone someone without appearing to be desperate. Nine o'clock on the dot was perhaps pushing his luck, so he decided to finish reading an article that he hadn't managed to get through the first time around.

He had almost finished when Sanna asked him to help her look for a film she couldn't find. By eleven minutes past nine, they had found the film and put it on, and Mike went out into the kitchen and phoned Nour.

Nour was Ylva's closest friend at work. Mike had only met her once, but immediately liked her. She had bright eyes and a smile that wasn't false.

'Hasn't she come home?' Nour asked.

'She said she was going out with you,' Mike said.

Nour didn't say anything for a beat, as if she was thinking about what she should say, and then realised that she couldn't lie.

'She told us that she was going home,' she said, eventually. 'Have you tried her mobile?'

'It's turned off.'

Nour could hear the suspicion in Mike's voice.

'Well, I've no idea then,' she said, and changed tack. 'I hope nothing's happened. Have you tried the hospital?'

'Wouldn't they have called me?'

Nour conceded.

'So, she said she was going home?' Mike repeated.

He immediately regretted his words, which sounded formal and accusing.

'Yes.'

'Did she say how she was going to get home?'

'By bus, I presume. We were out on the street and she walked off down the hill.'

'On her own?'

'Yes. We tried to persuade her to come with us, but she said she wanted to go home.'

'Okay, well, thanks for that.'

'Ask her to give me a call when she shows up,' Nour said.

'Of course,' Mike replied. 'We'll be in touch. Bye now.'

Ylva watched Mike collect the newspaper on the TV screen. She saw her husband come out in his dressing gown and get the newspaper from the postbox, as if nothing had happened.

What was he thinking? That she'd screwed someone, or crashed on a friend's sofa?

He must have phoned and tried to find out.

She caught a movement behind the sitting-room window. Mike had just gone in through the front door, so it must be Sanna. Ylva's daughter was so close and yet she couldn't go there.

Ylva twisted herself up off the bed. Her body ached and she smelled bad. She had pissed on the bed after he raped her, just lay there and let it run out. She hadn't showered, refused to, didn't want to think about using anything in this prison where she was being kept. That would mean accepting, giving in. And anyway, she would need to be examined by a doctor so the rape could be verified.

She went over to the door, balled her hands, shouted and hammered on it.

The noise she managed to create was muffled, as if the door was padded on the outside. But you should still be able to hear it on the other side, she thought.

A weapon. She needed to defend herself.

Ylva went through the drawers in the kitchenette. Plastic cutlery, a butter knife, cheese slicer, chopping boards, a roll of plastic bags. No knives, no metal cutlery, not even a tin opener. The cupboard over the sink was empty, except for a packet of crispbread and a stack of white plastic cups.

She searched the bathroom and found hand towels, soap and shampoo, laundry detergent, a hairbrush, lubricant and an emery board. Nothing that could be used. She went back out into the room and looked around.

The chair.

One of the legs could be used as a weapon, if she managed to break up the chair. She could swing it at them when they came in.

She got a firm hold of the back of the chair and smashed it against the wall. She repeated the procedure until one of the legs snapped, then she kicked it loose from the rest of the chair.

She sat down on the bed with the chair leg and looked at it. The broken end was sharp and jagged.

A weapon.

Mike wanted to ring his mum. He wanted to ring his mum and get her to explain, so he could understand. He had tried to be a good husband, made an effort every day, barely thought of anything else. Was that the problem maybe? The excessive desire to please?

Mike thought he'd managed to tone it down.

Was he annoying? Maybe he was; in fact, he was sure he was. And yet they'd had fun together, found things to do.

Why was she doing this? Why was she treating him like this? But what if something had happened? He could phone the hospital, maybe, just to ask. To be sure. To have something to do.

He went out into the sitting room, looked at his daughter. She was engrossed in what was going on on the screen. Animated, exaggerated and fast, with breathless voices.

He went back to the kitchen, closed the door quietly behind him. He phoned the operator, asked to be put through to the hospital. The woman on the switchboard then put him through to A&E where he rather sheepishly explained why he was calling, and was told that no one called Ylva Zetterberg had been admitted, no women of her age, in fact.

The woman he spoke to could hear how distressed he was.

'I'm sure she'll be back soon,' she said to encourage him. 'There'll be a perfectly reasonable explanation. My guess is that she's sleeping it off at a friend's.'

'Probably.'

'Well, she certainly hasn't had an accident,' the nurse repeated, 'because then we'd know about it.'

'Thank you. Thank you so much for your time.'

'Not at all. Have a good day.'

He dialled Nour's number again. She obviously hadn't had any problems going back to sleep after Mike's first call.

'It's me again. Sorry to disturb you.'

'No problem,' Nour said, still half asleep. 'Has she come back?'

'I called the hospital. She wasn't there.'

'Good.'

'Yes, but I'm getting quite worried now. You don't know if she might've gone out with some other people?'

The silence was a tenth of a second too long.

'She said she was going home.'

'Nour, sorry if I'm being too direct, but you must know that we had some problems a year or so ago.'

'She said she was going home,' Nour repeated.

'But she hasn't come home, so she obviously didn't.'

'No.'

'No what?'

'No, she can't have gone home,' Nour said.

'Do you know where she is?' Mike asked. 'You don't need to say anything to me, all I'm asking you to do is to ring her and get her to contact me. She just needs to let me know she's okay.'

'Look, she said she was going home.'

'Okay, okay.'

'I promise, I don't know anything,' Nour exclaimed. 'What time is it?'

'Nearly ten.'

'It's early yet. She'll come home. Maybe she met some friends on the way back and stayed out late with them, then crashed on someone's sofa, you know how it is. I'm sure there's a good reason.'

'Yes,' Mike muttered.

'Well, obviously nothing's happened.'

'No.'

'Because then she'd be in hospital,' Nour assured him.

'Right.'

'She'll be home in an hour, I promise.'

Mike said nothing. Nour wondered if he was crying.

'Um, Mike . . . ' she said, as gently as she could.

'I can't bear this,' he burst out. 'Can't bear it.'

'Mike, listen to me. Don't imagine the worst, there's no reason to. I'm sure it was just a late night, so she didn't want to call and wake you, and then she crashed and she's still asleep . . . She hasn't texted you?'

'No.'

His voice was so thin that Nour could barely hear it.

'Her phone's switched off,' he added with a sob.

'Maybe the battery's low,' Nour tried. 'I'm sure there's a thousand explanations. Do you want me to ring round and see what I can find out?'

'Please.'

'Okay, I'll do that. No matter what the explanation is, she should have let you know. And you don't need to feel stupid. D'you hear me? She's the one who's mucked up, not you. Okay?'

14

Starvation

Particularly non-compliant women are often starved. The lack of food dramatically reduces their ability to resist. Eventually, the woman does not have the energy to fight back, no matter what is done to her.

Ylva sat on the bed and stared at the screen. Holst drove past in his beautifully cared for old Volvo estate. There was a certain status in only buying a new car every twenty years, then driving it into the ground. It showed stability, old money and a healthy disregard for keeping up appearances.

Two schoolgirls, a couple of years older than Sanna,

cycled past down the middle of the road. They stood up on the pedals, rested a while, then cycled on.

Gunnarsson walked past with a light step and his white dog on a lead.

The small, respectable neighbourhood came to life. Everything was as normal. There was no evident activity inside or outside Ylva's house.

She stared at the screen, transfixed, the only window she had on the world outside.

The camera was set up on the second floor of the house, pointing down towards Ylva and Mike's house. The picture showed the street, the grassy area between Gröntevägen and Sundsliden where the children didn't play football and rounders often enough, and the start of Bäckavägen.

For long periods, nothing happened. The branches on the trees moved in the wind, nothing more. Then a car or a jogger might pass. But mostly cars, probably on their way to the shop to get whatever was needed for a perfect weekend breakfast. Fresh rolls, Tropicana juice, cheese.

Ylva felt dizzy. She hadn't eaten since lunch yesterday and had drunk barely a drop.

She went over to the kitchenette, still holding the jagged chair leg in her hand, and drank some water straight from the tap. She had to stop to breathe between gulps. She took out the crispbread and the Primula, squeezed it on generously, and stood by the sink while she ate.

The food gave her energy that spread through her body. The graininess disappeared from her eyes and she tried to convince herself that it was important to think clearly. Not to feel, but to think.

She didn't know what they wanted or had planned. Had they thought of keeping her there? Was she going to be kept prisoner in the cellar?

The thought grew and made her head spin with fear. She had to talk to them, find out, make them see sense. Hadn't they achieved what they wanted by raping her? Eye for an eye, tooth for a tooth. Why was she still here in this room?

This cellar ... they had bought a house and sound-proofed the cellar. They had fitted a kitchenette and bathroom, made a room within a room.

This was no sudden impulse, it was an expensive and well-executed plan.

They intended to keep her locked up.

Nour sighed loudly to herself. What did it have to do with her? Absolutely nothing.

It was Ylva's own fault. She was so needy, which was why she fucked around, and she should be ashamed.

And that crybaby, who didn't get anything. Didn't he realise he was a laughing stock?

Why the hell had Nour offered to ring round? Who was she going to call? And what was the point?

Hi, it's Nour. Is Ylva there?

No. Why would she be?

Mike phoned. She obviously didn't come home last night.

Whoops.

So you don't know anything?

No.

Everyone would hook into it like the busybodies they were and the word would soon spread.

Apparently Ylva didn't go home last night. Really? Wonder where she's sleeping then? Hehe.

Nour was trapped. There was nothing she could do. No matter how she looked at it, the result would simply add insult to injury and Mike was the loser.

And in any case, Ylva would be home soon enough, ashamed and pleading.

Never again. I promise.

Nour sat down on the bed, flopped back and stared up at the ceiling.

'Ylva Ylva Ylva Ylva . . . ' she muttered to herself.

Most beautiful women didn't seek attention, certainly not from men lower down the social, sexual or financial ladder. Ylva, on the other hand, couldn't get enough. If there was a man there, she had her eye on him. The fact that that made it impossible for women to be friends with her didn't bother her in the slightest.

As was so often the case with flirts, the attraction was a game, not real. And in most cases, it went no further than flirting and a bit of petting. The only man that Nour knew for certain Ylva had slept with was Bill Åkerman.

Nour didn't know much about him except that he'd wasted all the money his rich mother had invested in his stupid projects. It was only once his mother died that Bill, against the odds, managed to get a luxury restaurant up and running.

Nour was practically certain that Ylva was with him.

15

Mike cleared away the breakfast things, then took a shower. He closed his eyes and let the warm water stream over his face. The sound of the shower blocked out the rest of the world and made him realise that he couldn't carry on living like this.

He contemplated divorce, imagined that he would push it all through with extreme generosity in order to avoid any problems with custody. He thought he could get himself a second-floor flat with a balcony on the northside, with the water stretching out below. An every-second-week agreement? It had its advantages.

He pictured a new and healthier lifestyle. He would be sociable, not just sit there quietly any more, nodding and smiling.

Internet dating? There were plenty more fish in the sea.

A sound outside the shower made him immediately turn off the water. He got out and opened the bathroom door.

'Hello?' he shouted.

No reply.

'Ylva?'

Just the distant sound of Sanna's cartoon.

'Sanna!'

'What?'

'Did someone come in?'

'What?'

'Has Mummy come back?' Mike shouted at the top of his voice.

'No.'

'It just sounded like someone came in.'

'No.'

'Okay.'

Mike dried himself and got dressed, went down to Sanna in the sitting room. Watched her as she dragged her eyes reluctantly from the screen and looked at him questioningly.

'Thought we could go to Väla,' he said, quickly.

He hated the shopping centre, especially on a Saturday, but he was too restless to potter around at home, waiting for the homecoming queen.

'Now?'

'Yes, before there are too many people.'

'Can't we wait until Mummy comes home?'

'No, let's go now.'

The remote control was lying on the table. He picked it up.

'Go and put some clothes on.'

'But stop the film. I want to watch the rest when we get back.'

Sanna jumped down from the sofa and ran to her room. Mike switched to teletext and skimmed over the various listings and headlines. Nothing interesting, he decided, and turned it off.

He went out into the kitchen, took a piece of paper from Sanna's play box and wrote CALL ME on it. He left the piece of paper in the middle of the table, where it was visible.

Mike and Sanna left the house.

Ylva sat on the bed and stared at the screen. She saw her husband and daughter get into the car and drive away.

Ylva couldn't see everything in detail, but their movements were familiar and it wasn't difficult for her mind to fill in what her eyes couldn't see. The normal movements, seen a thousand times before, nothing dramatic. The front door opened. Sanna ran over to the car. Stood waiting by the passenger door, having obviously been promised she could sit next to Mike. Mike locked the front door, turned off the car alarm from a distance. They got in. Mike helped to belt in his daughter. He shut the car door. The red backlights went on. The car reversed out, stopped a moment before accelerating forward. Left into Bäckavägen, then left again up Sundsliden.

Ylva knew there was no point, but still screamed in loud desperation when she saw the top of the car pass by outside.

They'd gone out. What did that mean? Who had Mike contacted? What did he think?

It was quite easy to imagine what he was thinking. Maybe he couldn't stand waiting. Or he was driving Sanna over to his mother's as a precautionary measure. So that she wasn't there for the fight that Mike thought was in the offing.

Why didn't he ring the police? Or had he phoned them and been told to wait?

She will come home, just wait and see.

The officer on duty that he'd spoken to would then put down the phone and roll his eyes at a colleague and pour another cup of coffee.

Sanna had skipped down to the car as usual. She had no idea.

It was harder to guess what Mike was feeling. One of his most distinguishing traits was the fear of losing control, even though at heart he was a crybaby. Mike was far more a victim of his gender than Ylva had ever been.

He must at least have phoned the hospital. She would have done that. If nothing else, for tactical reasons, a means of reproach.

I even phoned the hospital.

A double martyr. Considerate and betrayed.

'Why do you keep looking at your mobile?'

Sanna sent her dad an accusing look.

'I don't.' He smiled sheepishly.

'You do, all the time.'

'I'm just checking to see if Mummy's called.'

'Where is she?'

'I don't really know.'

'Don't you know where she is?'

Sanna found that hard to understand and Mike felt the tears well up in his eyes.

'All I know is that she's out with her friends. That is to say, she was. They went out together yesterday. They were probably out late, so she stayed over with one of them.'

'But she hasn't phoned?'

'Look!' Mike said, and pointed out to the right.

Sanna turned around and Mike swiftly wiped the corners of his eyes.

'What?' Sanna asked.

'The bird, the big bird over there.'

'Where?'

'Oh, it's flown away.'

'I didn't see a bird.'

'Didn't you? It was a big one, maybe an eagle. Have you ever seen an eagle? They look like a flying door. Mummy will be home soon. I'm sure she'll be there waiting for us, when we get back from Väla.'

'I still think she could phone,' Sanna said.

16

I can't say that I'm sorry.

Jörgen's words had engraved themselves in Calle Collin's mind. The worst thing was that they were spontaneous. Jörgen hadn't said it to be mean, it was an instinctive reaction to the news that Anders Egerbladh had been murdered.

Calle looked up the hammer murder on the Internet. After surfing for half an hour, he had the basic facts. Anders Egerbladh, who all the articles stated was thirty-six, had been beaten to death on Sista Styverns Trapp, a flight of wooden steps that went from Fjällgatan up to

Stigbergsgatan. The murder weapon, a hammer, had been left at the scene of the crime, but had no fingerprints on it.

The murder was described as bestial. The level of violence indicated an intense hate for the victim, and the police were working on the hypothesis that the victim and the killer knew each other. A bunch of flowers had been found at the scene, which was assumed to indicate that the thirty-six-year-old had been on his way to visit a woman. And reading between the lines, a married woman.

The best articles were written by a crime reporter from an evening paper where Calle Collin had once wasted six months of his professional life. He got the feeling that the reporter knew more than he was sharing with his readers. Calle didn't know the journalist personally, but he did know one of the editors. If she put a word in for him, he might be able to talk to the reporter.

Calle had worked as a temp on the paper's women's page, where all the articles were based on the first commandment of McCarthy feminism: that there was no difference between men and women, except that men are by nature evil and women are by nature good.

Headlines and angles were pre-set and the editorial work

consisted simply of putting together arguments that backed the claim and eliminating anything that might oppose it. Without so much as batting an eye, journalists on the page took to task anyone who dared to question their machinations in the name of the cause.

The fact that many of those who were hounded, and whose lives and actions were scorned, were in fact good role models for equality was neither here nor there if they so much as hinted, in even a subclause, that they may have a different opinion.

All in all, this meant that what were essentially important questions were often ridiculed, and those six months working at the supplement had instilled in Calle Collin a permanent distrust of public debate. The only positive thing about his time there was that he had got to know one of the editors, a wise woman with a big heart. When Calle had had enough after six months, she asked whether he would perhaps prefer to go down to the news desk.

'If I was interested in news, I would've gone to a newspaper,' Calle had replied.

For a long time after, he was frequently quoted by the editorial team. Most people laughed, even agreed with him, but the arts editor was furious and had sworn that, as far as he could, he would make sure that Calle never set foot in the place again.

Calle picked up the receiver and dialled the wise woman with the big heart.

17

The uglier a place was, the more people thronged there. The national parks were almost deserted, but every revolting shopping centre in the country was full to bursting with people with no taste, empty eyes and a fat wallet.

And nowhere was worse or more repulsive than Väla shopping centre. And yet Mike went there at least once a week. Because you could get everything there, even free parking. Just load the car and drive home.

Ylva was happy to wander round the same shops, week-end in and weekend out, and with a keen eye pick out the new things from the vast range of what was on offer. Mike, on the other hand, hurried through the indoor streets that had sprung up, terrified that the rubbish would stick to him.

Sanna was somewhere in between. The pet shop was an attraction, as was the ice-cream stall and all the people.

The hustle and bustle, sounds and impressions, were the highlight of the week for many.

Ylva would lay her newly purchased finds out on the bed when she got home, as if they were prey or a trophy. Admiring her own skill. She'd tell Sanna what she'd bought, why she'd bought it and how the various new items of clothing could be combined with the ones she already had.

Mike wondered whether it was some kind of training, whether that was how new consumers were generated.

And he certainly didn't have the peace of mind to wander round and pretend that nothing was wrong now.

'So, what do you reckon, sweetheart? McDonald's and then home?'

'But we've just got here.'

'Well, aren't you hungry?'

'Not really.'

'Okay, let's go round the shops a bit and then we can have a bite to eat. Okay?'

Ylva still hadn't called and a nagging worry was starting to keep his anger company.

The thought that something might have happened, that there was a legitimate reason why she hadn't phoned, was almost comforting. Being worried was easier than being frightened.

But he was frightened, frightened of being dumped and written out of the plot.

At least as a consoler – or, God forbid, a mourner – Mike would have a role to play.

Sanna chewed slowly and surveyed the world around her with big eyes, and in here that meant overweight families, dirty tables and stressed staff.

Mike had finished his food and was bouncing his foot nervously under the table.

'You enjoying that?'

He smiled at his daughter and did his best to hide the fact that he would happily pay a substantial part of his salary if he could leave the place immediately. McDonald's was their last stop. They had been to the pet shop, browsed through the DVDs in the bookshop and looked for cheap jewellery in the accessories shop.

Sanna nodded, took a bite of a fry. Everything was slow. Mike had finished before his daughter had even picked the gherkin out of her burger.

'If you concentrate on your burger, then maybe we could take the fries with us,' he said and forced a smile.

'Are we in a hurry?'

'What? Um, no. We're not in a hurry.'

Sanna chewed her deep-fried potato thoughtfully as two little boys at the next table squabbled over the toys they'd got with their happy meal.

Mike resigned himself to the fact that he had at least another half-hour of torture ahead of him.

He got his mobile out from the inside pocket of his jacket, checked the screen to make sure that he hadn't missed any calls and tried Ylva again. Straight to voicemail. He hung up without leaving a message. He dialled the house and let it ring about six times before ending the call.

He looked at his daughter and then held the phone up with the exaggerated explanation of a parent.

'I have to make a phone call,' he said. 'I'll be standing just over there where I can see you. Okay?'

'Can't you ring from here?' Sanna asked.

'There's someone I need to talk to.'

'But you just phoned someone.'

'That was someone else. I don't want there to be a lot of noise in the background. Just sit where you are, I'll be right outside.'

He went to the door, waved over at his daughter and dialled Nour's number.

'Hi, it's Mike.'

'Hi, has she shown up yet?'

'No, she hasn't. At least, I don't think so. I'm at Väla with Sanna, but I left a note to say she should call. And she hasn't. And there's no answer on her mobile or at home. Have you heard anything?'

'Well . . . I . . . Nothing much, no, but I'll carry on. I'll let you know if I do hear anything.'

'Okay, thanks. And, Nour, listen . . . '

'Yes?'

'Well, if she is . . . you know, if she has done something stupid, well, I'd still like to hear from her. It doesn't feel right like this. I'm getting worried.'

Nour rang the restaurant that was owned by Ylva's ex-lover. It was just after one and she guessed that they would be open. She said who she was and asked to speak to Bill

Åkerman. Luckily he was there, which lowered the chances that he'd spent the night with Ylva or knew where she was, but Nour wanted to make sure.

'Hello.'

His voice was aggressive, just like his personality.

'Hello, my name is Nour. I work with Ylva Zetterberg.'

Bill waited for her to finish and to say more.

'I've seen you a couple of times,' Nour continued. 'But I don't think you know who I am.'

'I know who you are.'

His voice was cold and businesslike, there was no hint of invitation or intimacy. But Nour still felt flattered in a way. She wondered whether Bill's success with women was simply due to social ineptitude. Or was it disinterest? Bill didn't care, which aroused a competitive spirit in women who were normally spoilt for attention.

'I'm sorry to call you like this, but it's kind of urgent. Ylva's disappeared. She didn't go home last night. Her husband's called me a couple of times and asked if I maybe know where she is.'

'I have no idea.'

'So she wasn't with you?'

'Why the hell would she be?'

'I know that you—'

'That was a hundred years ago. Was there anything else?'

'No.'

Bill hung up. Nour sat with the telephone in her hand. Her immediate impulse was to go to the restaurant and apologise. She didn't feel good, like an old gossip sniffing out scandal.

Ylva would be furious when she found out that Nour had phoned Bill.

Nour was ashamed. She had let herself be drawn in by Mike's anxiety. Instead of reassuring him, she had taken his hysteria a step further.

Did Mike even know that his wife had had an affair with Bill? Nour wasn't certain.

If Ylva didn't turn up soon, Mike would ring her again to find out who she'd spoken to. She couldn't really say that the only person she'd contacted was Bill. Nour had to phone a few other people, so she could say that she had. Despite the fact that she already knew that none of them would have any idea where Ylva might be. The phone calls would only reinforce the image of Nour as some hysterical gossipmonger.

Nour felt her irritation growing. How come she should be tidying up after Ylva? She wasn't the one who'd fucked around.

109

18

Sanna saved the longest fries until last.

'Look,' she said, holding one up in front of her.

'Wow, that's a long one,' Mike said.

He glanced over quickly and then looked back at the road. He stayed in lane on the roundabout and out on to the motorway.

'I've had longer ones,' Sanna said, world weary. 'One was super long.'

'Longer than that?' Mike exclaimed.

'Much longer. Double as long.'

'Really?'

'Well, maybe not double.'

'But very long?'

'Yes.'

Sanna happily stuffed the fry in her mouth.

Mike wondered whether he should drive into town and ask his mother to look after Sanna for a couple of hours. That would leave him free to make phone calls and do some ferreting, and it would spare Sanna having to witness the scene when Ylva finally decided to pitch up. The problem would obviously be his mother's questions and accusations. She and Ylva rubbed along well enough, but their friendliness was strained, and he didn't want to upset the balance.

Mike should probably contact the police. Not because he thought it was necessary, but because Ylva deserved it. It made it seem more serious and reinforced the idea that he'd been taken in. The alternative, that he suspected her of being unfaithful without doing anything about it, was worse.

He decided to go home. It was more than likely that Ylva would be waiting for them there.

Mike managed to convince himself and took the northbound exit at Berga.

*

The front door was still locked and there were no new shoes in the hall. But Mike called anyway.

'Hello?'

Sanna looked up at him.

'Is Mummy still not home?'

Mike shook his head.

'Where is she?'

'I don't know.'

'You don't know.'

Mike didn't reply.

'Has she vanished?'

Sanna said it as a joke.

'No, no, not vanished,' Mike said, and forced a smile. 'She's somewhere. Obviously.'

'But where is she then?'

'Probably with a friend.'

He looked at his watch. Quarter to two.

'I have to make some phone calls,' he said.

'You keep making phone calls all the time.'

'I have to. You don't want to go and play with a friend?'

'Who?'

'Klara, maybe?'

'She's not at home.'

'What about Ivan?'

'I want to wait for Mummy.'

'Go and watch a film then, please. I'll come through as soon as I've made my phone calls.'

Sanna sighed and disappeared.

Mike waited until he heard the sound of a film, then phoned Nour.

'Who have you spoken to?' he asked, when she explained that no one knew anything.

'Pia and Helena,' Nour said. 'I don't know who else to contact.'

Mike mustered his courage.

'Could she be with that restaurant muppet?'

He forced a laugh when he said it, as if he wanted to joke away his only real question as something unthinkable.

'No,' she said. 'I phoned him too, just to make sure. They haven't met.'

Mike felt relieved even though he knew that that meant his wife was possibly being unfaithful with someone else.

'What time did she leave you yesterday?' Mike asked.

Nour took a deep breath and released it in a sigh.

'I think it was quarter past six or thereabouts.'

'So she would have been back by seven, if she'd come straight home,' Mike calculated.

'Yes, I guess.'

'And she went down the hill?'

'She said she was going home.'

'I think I'd better call the police,' Mike said.

Nour thought he sounded a bit embarrassed, almost as if he was asking her permission. She didn't know what to say. Mike filled the silence himself.

'I had a mate in Stockholm who pissed on the palace once. He'd been to Café Opera and was shambling along Skeppsbron when he had to take a leak. Which he did, not very carefully, by the fountain. The police kept him in overnight, he wasn't even allowed to phone home. His girlfriend was waiting for him with the rolling pin, thought he'd been sleeping around.'

The story was irrelevant and his voice was forced, as if he was trying to convince himself. Mike was about to crack.

'I mean, it might be something like that.'

Yes, Nour thought to herself, if Ylva was a man and there was a palace to piss on, it might.

'Absolutely,' she said. 'Of course it might. I think it's best that you call the police.'

'Just to be on the safe side,' Mike said.

19

Ylva stared at the screen. Mike and Sanna were back, and the car was parked in front of the garage. Her beloved, patient and stubborn husband was sitting only a hundred metres away, wondering what had become of her. Ylva felt a physical longing to be there.

She pulled all the paper from the kitchen roll, let it fall in a pile on the floor. Then she took the empty roll and positioned herself on the bed. By directing the sound and shouting through the cardboard tube she hoped she could attract the attention of anyone passing. She waited in suspense, eyes on the TV screen.

When the first couple walked past, she shouted as loud as she could. Unfortunately a car drove past at the same time and drowned out what little noise she was able to make. The next person to pass was a jogger, with music in his ears, not worth the effort. Then an elderly couple who looked like they might stop, which made Ylva shout even more so that they'd realise that something was wrong. They actually stopped and looked at the house. Ylva was sure that they could hear her, without knowing where the sound was coming from, but they didn't look particularly concerned and after a while they carried on walking, despite her loud cries for help.

Of course they couldn't imagine that the couple who had recently moved in had locked someone up in the cellar.

Ylva tried to listen instead. She sat with the cardboard roll to her ear and pressed it up to the vent. She heard an electric fan, but nothing from outside. A couple of cars passed without the sound of the engine penetrating down into the cellar.

When finally Lennart, Virginia's pathetic husband, glided silently past on his Harley Davidson, which didn't have a silencer, she realised that the cellar room was cut off from the rest of the world, at least in terms of sound.

It was almost impossible to comprehend. That it was actually possible to build a cube under a house with air ventilation both in and out, and water, and yet not a sound could escape.

Ylva reminded herself to think constructively. So, she couldn't attract attention using her voice. Instead of wasting energy thinking about that, she had to come up with another solution.

If she'd had a lighter or matches, she could set fire to the kitchen roll and let the smoke seep out through the vent and attract someone's attention that way. The disadvantage of that would be that she risked burning to death or inhaling smoke, and if the vent opened into the chimney pipe, the smoke wouldn't make anyone react, not even now, when it was warm outside. People would assume that the new couple were burning rubbish in the fireplace and not think any more of it.

And it was perfectly feasible that the vent was connected to the chimney. That would explain why her cries couldn't be heard.

What else then? Fire, air . . . water.

There was water in the bathroom. It came in via the pipes and disappeared down the drain. Could she flush down some kind of waterproof message in the hope that someone at the sewage works would notice it? She pictured the tampons, condoms and rubbish in a revolting sludge of shit and toilet paper. No one would be exactly tempted to look any closer.

Paper. What about if she blocked the toilet so it over-flowed? They'd be forced to open the door then.

She heard a sound outside. A key being inserted in the lock of the metal door that separated her from the outside world.

She looked around, grabbed the broken chair leg and held it in front of her.

She was prepared.

The policeman who filed Mike's report over the phone was calm and understanding. He asked, without causing embar-rassment, whether Ylva had a history of being down or depressed, if she had disappeared before without getting in touch, whether Mike and Ylva had perhaps quarrelled or disagreed recently.

'So when she left her colleagues just after six, she said she was going home?' he asked, when Mike had finished.

'Yes.'

'And she said to you that she was going out?'

'She said that she might, but that nothing had been decided.'

'And when was the last time you spoke?'

'Yesterday morning, before she went to work.'

'And her mobile has been switched off?' the policeman probed.

Mike knew how it sounded. She'd spent the night with her lover. It had been wonderful and she didn't want to break the spell, only to replace it with broken crockery and feelings of guilt.

'Let me be frank,' the policeman said. 'We get calls like this more or less every day. And nearly always, the person reappears within twenty-four hours. Your wife has been missing for twenty hours now, so I suggest that if she hasn't been in touch by the evening, you call me again. I'm here until nine.'

The policeman gave him a direct number.

'One more thing,' he added. 'When she comes home, take it easy. Don't do anything stupid.'

'I won't,' Mike said, like an obedient schoolboy.

'Remember that tomorrow is another day.'

'Yes.'

Mike even nodded, standing there alone in the kitchen.

'Good,' the policeman said. 'Then I hope that I won't be hearing from you later. Take care. Goodbye.'

Mike put the receiver down and felt that he'd done the right thing. He'd phoned Nour, who had then phoned their friends and that slimeball of a restaurant owner. He'd contacted the hospital and now the police. There wasn't anything else he could do.

Mike went out to his daughter in the sitting room. She looked at him.

'When's Mummy coming home?'

'She'll be here soon. Any minute, I reckon.'

'Do you think she's bought anything?'

'What? No, I don't think so.'

Mike turned to look at the TV and hoped that Sanna would do the same. He didn't like her looking at him when he was weak.

The feeling that overwhelmed him now was guilt. His efficiency was swept to one side by a blast of regret. He'd run to the teacher and told tales. He could see Ylva's accusing eyes.

One bloody night. Couldn't she have one bloody night

off and let her hair down? Without him getting hysterical and behaving like an idiot.

'Do you want to build a tower?'

'Lego,' Sanna countered.

'Okay, Lego.'

20

Violence / threat of violence

**Violence and the threat of violence are constantly pres-
ent in the victim's life. A woman who continues to
resist is subjected to violence. In those cases where the
woman refuses to give in, the abuse can become so violent that it can lead to death.**

The man smiled when he opened the door and saw Ylva
holding the jagged chair leg up like a weapon in front of her.
It wasn't the reaction that Ylva had hoped for.

'Let me go,' she said.

She wished that her voice was stronger. The man closed
the door.

'I said LET ME GO!'

She sounded desperate now. The man didn't answer. The door clicked shut behind him. Ylva thrust the chair leg around in front of her, threatening.

'The key, give me the key!'

The man held the key ring out in front of him. He was finding it difficult to hide his amusement.

'Drop it on the floor.'

The man did what Ylva told him.

'Move away.'

She waved the chair leg at him.

'The kitchen?' he asked, and pointed towards the kitchenette.

Ylva realised that that wasn't a good idea. There wasn't enough distance to the door.

'The bathroom,' Ylva ordered, and backed away to give him room to pass.

He nodded and went in.

'Close the door behind you.'

He obeyed.

'And lock it,' Ylva shouted.

He locked it. Ylva looked around for something to jam the door, but there wasn't anything except the broken chair.

She bent down and picked up the key ring, without letting go of the chair leg. With shaking hands, she fumbled for the right key. There were two to choose from. Finally she managed to get the first one in, but couldn't turn it. She pulled out the key, dropped the key ring, bent down and picked it up again.

The second key didn't fit in the lock at all. She tried the first one again. Had just pushed it back into the lock when the bathroom door opened.

'Do you need some help?'

Ylva spun round, holding the chair leg in front of her with outstretched arms.

The man came out of the bathroom, put his hand into his pocket and pulled out a single key.

'Guess you've got the wrong ones,' he said.

'Give it to me!'

The man stepped back, smiled.

'You'll have to get it from me.'

Ylva went for him. She lifted her arms above her head and stormed towards him. He jumped nimbly up on to the bed.

'This is fun,' he said. 'Just like when we were children.'

'Let me out, you bastard.'

'Of course. But first you have to get the key.'

He held it out, teasing her. Ylva got up on to the bed, the man stayed where he was.

'Give it to me.'

'Here, take it.'

'Put it down,' Ylva ordered. 'Put the key down now.'

'Take it.'

'I'll hit you.'

'Come on then, take the key.'

Ylva swung the chair leg and hit him and gashed open his hand. He looked at the thin line that was now filling with blood.

'That hurt,' he said, and put the wound to his mouth and sucked.

'I'll hit you again,' Ylva screamed. 'I will. Give me the key. Now!'

The man stopped sucking. The amused look on his face had been replaced by anger.

'Okay, that's enough.'

He reached out to try to get the chair leg from Ylva. She hit him again, he grabbed her arm and blocked the movement. With his other hand, he wrestled the chair leg out of Ylva's grasp and threw it to one side, then forced her face down on to the bed.

'I'm going to have to teach you some fucking manners.'

He straddled her thighs and pulled down her jeans without undoing the buttons and started to spank her on the bottom. He hit her until she was red before pulling down her trousers completely and thrusting his hand into her vagina.

She heard him unbutton his own jeans.

Mike built up the Lego pieces along the edges of the base plate. Sanna was critical of his work.

'Aren't you going to have windows?'

'I can't find any.'

'You could just leave an opening. You can't get bored if there's a window.'

Mike looked at his little grown-up daughter. She noticed it.

'That's what the teacher says,' she explained. 'It's a saying or something.'

How like that hideous old witch, Mike thought to himself. She's not ashamed to ask the children what their parents do or what kind of car they've got. Mike had his own cynical version of the saying his daughter had just shared with him: *An ugly view is always ugly, a beautiful one only interesting for ten minutes.*

It was not an attitude to life that he wanted to hand down to Sanna.

'You're right,' he said, and removed some bricks. 'If you've got a window, you won't ever be bored.'

'And doors,' Sanna said. 'Otherwise you can't get in.'

'Or out,' Mike said.

'But you have to go in first.'

'Right again.'

Mike looked at the clock. Quarter to six.

'Is Mummy not coming home soon? I'm hungry.'

'She'll be here anytime now.'

Sanna gave a long sigh.

'We can get a pizza,' Mike suggested, and immediately felt a pang of remorse.

A burger and pizza on the same day, both as good as cake in terms of nourishment. Mike didn't care, things being what they were. It wasn't a day like any other.

He got up. His body was stiff. He didn't know if it was because he was tense or because he'd spent an hour and a half on the floor playing with Lego.

He went out into the kitchen. The pizza menu was stuck to the fridge with a magnet, a last resort on bad days when imagination and motivation were lacking.

'Cheese and ham?'

'The usual.'

Mike phoned and ordered.

'If we go straight away, we can buy some Saturday treats.'

Sanna scrambled to her feet.

'Can we get a film as well?'

'If we're quick. It would be a shame if the pizza got cold.'

Mike said that to be on the safe side. Sanna chose her films as if world peace depended on it. Even then, nine times out of ten, it was one she'd already seen. The comfort of familiarity.

21

Deprecation

Victims are constantly given negative feedback and brainwashed into believing that they lack human worth. The woman is scorned and denigrated, told that she is disgusting, a dirty whore, and that her body is only good for one thing. By means of verbal and physical abuse, the victim is robbed of the right to her own thoughts and body.

'Twice in less than twenty-four hours. We're practically a couple.'

Ylva wept silently, lying on her side, cheek to the covers, staring at the wall.

'And you were wet.'

He stood and buttoned up his trousers.

'I haven't even seen your breasts yet.'

He slapped her lightly on the calf.

'Turn over, I want to see your breasts.'

Ylva just lay there and didn't move. The man knelt one leg back down on the bed, grabbed her hip and turned her over.

'Your breasts. Don't make this any harder on yourself. You think I haven't seen breasts before?'

Ylva lifted up her top, turned her face away.

'Sit up so I can see. All breasts are flat when you're lying down.'

He sat her up and took a step back.

'Off with your top. Your bra as well, no messing around.'

He looked from left to right and back, with the expression of a disappointed horse trader.

'You're too thin,' he said eventually. 'All the women round here are. You'll need to put on a bit of weight. That might be difficult to begin with, with all the stress, but you'll soon get used to it.'

He sat down on the bed.

'Let me guess what you're thinking. You're trying to

work out how you can get out of here, you're thinking about how unfair it is that you're being kept here against your will. You keep watching the screen, waiting for something to happen, a dramatic event that will end in your release. It's natural.' He sat down on the bed. 'And believe me,' he continued, 'I don't want to interfere with your dreams and fantasies. But the sooner you accept your situation, the easier it will be.'

He put his finger under her chin and lifted her head. She met his eyes, without reciprocating his smile.

'You're sick,' she said.

The man shrugged.

'If you did manage to escape, which I strongly doubt, I'd be in the headlines for weeks, of course I would. But, you see, when you've suffered misfortune and loss, life changes. Things that were once important become meaningless and what you thought of as nonsense before suddenly becomes an obsession.'

He patted her on the arm and stood up.

'You'll be grateful for the small things. It might be hard to imagine now, but I promise you, you'll get there. And we'll make the journey together.'

*

They ate the pizza straight from the box.

'Don't forget the salad,' Mike nagged.

'I don't like pizza salad,' Sanna complained.

Mike dropped it. He'd attempted an enticing *Milk?* as he set the table, but capitulated to the very clear reply: *It's Saturday*.

Mike had cut Sanna's pizza into smaller pieces and she ate while she looked at the DVD cover for *The Parent Trap*, a film about twins who've grown up not knowing about each other, one with the mother in England and the other with the father in the USA. After meeting at a summer camp, they switch places. When the father decides to marry a gold-digger, the twins set about stopping the plans.

The best kind of film, according to Sanna. Mike was forced to agree.

The grease dripped from Sanna's pizza.

'Here,' Mike said, and handed her a piece of kitchen roll. 'It's dripping.'

Sanna took it and wiped herself awkwardly. Mike was about to give her a hand when he suddenly remembered his own father's irritated comment: *Can't you feel that you've got sticky fingers?*

'Just wash your hands when you're finished,' he said, gently.

'Okay.'

As usual, Mike was done before Sanna had even finished her first slice. He insisted that she have one more, which he put on to her plate. Then he put his glass and cutlery into the dishwasher and went out to throw the boxes straight in the bin.

Helsingborg local council had introduced an over-ambitious environmental project that involved all residents sorting their rubbish down to an atomic level. It was a minor science now with a dozen different plastic bins, which had in turn made the binmen so self-important and difficult that they refused to empty any bins that were not right at the edge of the pavement well before they did their rounds.

Mike ripped the boxes into small pieces and then stood for a while outside the house, breathing in the fresh air, completely unaware that his wife was not far away, watching him on a grainy TV screen, with tears in her eyes.

22

'I take it that you're not going to write about the case?'

Erik Bergman looked at Calle Collin in amusement. The meeting had been arranged by the wise woman with the big heart, and she had also reminded the crime reporter that Calle was the temp who some years earlier had said no to a job on the evening paper's news desk, with the now infamous words: *If I was interested in news, I would've gone to a newspaper.*

'Anders Egerbladh and I were in the same class,' Calle said.

Erik Bergman nodded with interest.

'And what was he like?'

'An arse.'

'Serial shagger was what I was told,' Bergman said.

'I'm sure, that too,' Calle replied. 'Though I can't honestly say that I ever met him as an adult. Maybe he changed . . .'

Erik Bergman looked at him sceptically.

'. . . became a good person,' Calle said. 'But I find that hard to believe.'

'What is it that you want to know?' Bergman asked.

'I read your articles on the Internet,' Calle explained, 'and I may have got the wrong end of the stick, but I had a feeling that you knew more than you wrote.'

'Why do you want to know?'

Calle shrugged and shook his head at the same time.

'Curious. It sounds so dramatic: "The hammer murder", "bestial".'

'In this case, they were the right words. We had a bit of a problem with the tag line. We played with The Murder on Fjällgatan or The Steps Murder, as we'd already used The Hammer Murder a few times before. But it was undeniably gruesome. As I said, Anders Egerbladh liked to put it around. There were some divorcees, but most of the women he met via the dating sites were married. I don't know if he got a kick from it or whether married women use the Internet more. Whatever, it took half the police force to question all the spouses.'

'And . . .?'

'Nope, nothing. They went through all his phone records and email history and discovered that he'd arranged to meet a woman at Gondolen. Then she called at the last minute, presumably to ask him to come to her place instead. After the conversation, he left the restaurant, bought a bunch of flowers from the stall down by Slussen and walked up towards Fjällgatan.'

'So it was a trap?'

'Without a doubt. The woman doesn't actually exist. She used a pay-as-you-go phone and all emails were sent from public computers around town. And the photos on the dating website were downloaded from a foreign blog.'

'I got the impression, from what I've read, that the violence was more, well, what can I say, like a man?'

Erik Bergman nodded.

'I think you'd do well in news,' he said. 'The police have worked on the assumption that the murder was carried out by a man, but that a woman was there to lure Anders Egerbladh to the right spot.'

'And they don't have any clues?'

'No. The only thing they know for certain is that the murder was carried out with great force.'

23

When Mike went back into the house after he'd put the pizza boxes in the bin, he realised he was no longer in any doubt. He knew what he had to do.

He carefully pulled the door between the kitchen and the sitting room to, and dialled the number.

'Kristina.'

'Hi, Mum.'

Mike explained as briefly as he could that Ylva had been missing for more than twenty-four hours, and that none of her friends or the hospital or the police knew where she was.

'Could something have happened?' she asked.

'I don't know,' Mike said. 'But could you jump in a taxi and come over here, and stay until Ylva gets back?'

Twenty minutes later, Kristina arrived with a distressed expression. She said a quick and forced hello to Sanna before she joined her son in the kitchen. She had a thousand questions.

'I don't know, Mum,' was Mike's answer to each of them. 'I don't know.'

'Do you think she ... '

Mike held up his hands and closed his eyes in irritation.

'Mum, I don't know anything. Can you please just keep Sanna company while I phone the police?'

It was too late. Sanna was already standing in the doorway.

'Why are you phoning the police?' she asked.

Mike went over to her, bent down and smiled, to stop himself from crying.

'I don't know where Mummy is.'

Sanna didn't understand and looked at her grandmother, puzzled. As if she were a more reliable source of information than Daddy.

'Has she disappeared?'

Mike answered for his mother.

'No, no,' he said. 'She hasn't disappeared. She has to be somewhere, of course. But she hasn't phoned and I want to know where she is. There's nothing to be frightened of. If you and Granny go and watch a film, then I can make some phone calls.'

'But I want Mummy to come home.'

'Mummy will come home,' Kristina said. 'That's why Daddy has to make some phone calls. Come on, poppet, why don't you and I go and watch a film.'

She held out her hand and Sanna started to cry. Mike scooped her up and held her tight.

'There, there, sweetie, there's no need to be frightened. Mummy will be home soon. There's nothing to worry about. Mummy will be here soon.'

They sat round the kitchen table. Mike had offered them coffee, but the officers had declined, given that it was late. The policewoman asked for a glass of water. Kristina got her one and then stood leaning against the worktop like an observer. Sanna sat silently on her father's knee and solemnly listened to the conversation.

The policewoman smiled at her. The man asked the questions and wrote down the answers.

'Okay, let me summarise: your wife left work just after six o'clock yesterday evening and then disappeared?'

Mike nodded.

The policeman looked down at his notes and continued: 'She said to her colleagues that she was going home. But she'd told you that she was going to go for a drink with her colleagues?'

The policeman put his pen down on the notepad and looked up at Mike without raising his head.

'I know how it sounds, but that's not the case. She said that she *might* go out for a glass of wine. She said that before she left in the morning.'

'Does she often go out with her colleagues?'

'They had a final proof. And that can take a while. She probably thought she wouldn't be home in time for supper.'

'So you got worried when she didn't come home.'

Mike shook his head.

'I assumed that she was out with her friends.'

'Did you try to call her?'

'Not until later, I didn't want to . . .'

The policewoman folded her hands on the table in front of her and leaned forward with interest.

'You didn't want to what?'

'Well, I thought that you have to be able to go out on your own sometimes, even when you're married. We trust each other.'

'So you didn't think . . .?'

The woman chose not to finish the question, out of consideration to Sanna.

'No,' Mike replied.

There was a brief pause, which was long enough for Kristina to understand.

'Sanna, darling, I think Daddy needs to talk to the police alone for a while. Let's go and brush our teeth in the meantime, shall we?'

'But I want to know too.'

Mike lifted Sanna down from his lap.

'I'll be there soon, sweetie.'

'She's my mummy,' Sanna complained.

Mike and the police officers gave her an encouraging smile and waited until she had left the kitchen. They heard her continue to complain and her grandmother's wise, calm answers through the door.

Mike leaned forward and looked from the man to the woman.

'Ylva normally phones,' Mike explained. 'She always

phones. Sometimes she comes home late, it has happened before. And of course we've had our problems, just like everyone else. But, and this is important, she always phones.'

'Your problems,' the policewoman probed. 'Were you thinking of anything in particular?'

Mike controlled himself. He couldn't afford to be rude. 'No,' he said.

Mike took over as soon as the police had left. It was the first time that Sanna had distanced herself from her grandmother and demonstrated that she wasn't good enough.

Mike lay down beside his daughter, stroked her hair and comforted her as best he could. He was sure that Mummy would be home again soon, he said. He was sure that there hadn't been an accident, because he'd spoken to the hospital several times. Mummy wasn't hurt.

'Are you going to get divorced?'

'Why would we do that?'

'Vera's parents are getting divorced,' Sanna told him. 'Her daddy disappeared.'

'I see. No, we're going to stay together. At least, I hope we are.'

Sanna started to run her finger along the pattern in the wallpaper and fifteen minutes later she was asleep. Mike left the door wide open and went down to his mother in the kitchen.

'I hope you're not upset,' he said.

'No, no, no,' she assured him, 'it's only natural.'

'What's the time?'

He looked at his watch and answered his own question.

'Eleven.'

'I'll make some coffee,' his mother said. 'I'm sure we won't sleep anyway.'

Mike sat at the kitchen table, his hands clenched, eyes staring ahead. His lips moved to form words, but there was no sound. Kristina poured two cups of coffee and sat down opposite him.

'Will you stay with her after this?' she asked.

He gave her a stern look.

'Mother, we don't know what's happened.'

She turned away.

'No. No, we don't. That's right.'

She tasted the coffee, put her cup down, and let silence fill the room.

'Who have you spoken to?' she asked, finally.

'Nour.'

'From Ylva's work?'

'Yes. Plus Anders and Ulrika, Björn and Grethe, Bengtsson.'

'And no one knows anything?'

'No.'

Kristina fidgeted, uncomfortable with the question she was about to ask.

'What about you know who . . .?'

In a weak moment, Mike had told his mother of Ylva's affair with Bill Åkerman, mainly because he had no one else to confide in. He had regretted it bitterly later and felt that his betrayal was almost worse than Ylva's.

Mike looked his mother in the eye.

'No,' he said. 'Nour phoned him. She hasn't been there.'

Kristina changed tack.

'Who else could you phone?'

'I don't want to ring anyone else. It's bad enough as it is. And considering that I spoke to Bengtsson only two hours ago, it wouldn't surprise me if everyone else already knows what's happened.'

'I was thinking more about her workplace.'

'I've spoken to Nour,' Mike said. 'She's her best friend.'

'Exactly,' his mother replied. 'She's Ylva's best friend.'

'Mum, stop. She should damn well have phoned. It's not as if she's scared of me.'

'No, Lord only knows.'

'What's that supposed to mean?'

Kristina looked down at the table, ran her finger along the edge.

'Sorry,' she said. 'That was a stupid thing to say. I apologise.'

Mike took a deep breath, held it in.

'Mum, I need your support more than your help. Your support, Mum.'

24

Debt

Many victims are forced to work to pay off a debt. They have to pay for their journey, accommodation, bed, condoms, and a percentage to the perpetrator for his protection. This debt is naturally a construction. The victim will never be able to buy herself free. Her only option is to become unprofitable, which in practice is impossible as there will always be preferences that need to be met, something that she is suitable for.

The man and the woman came in together. They flung open the door and didn't bother to close it behind them. Ylva was lying on the bed, where she'd fallen asleep with her clothes on. It took a few seconds, a moment of confusion, before she realised that her dream wasn't real, unlike the hell she now found herself in.

The man and the woman positioned themselves on either side of the bed. Ylva tried to get away from the man, and ended up by the woman. The woman was smaller than Ylva, but this was not about size. The woman hit her hard across the face with her open hand. At the same time, the man gripped Ylva's ankles and pulled her over to him. Ylva fell on to her stomach, grabbed hold of the edge of the bed and struggled to resist him.

'We'll teach you to try to escape,' the woman said, and unclenched her fingers.

The man pulled her towards him without any difficulty, got hold of her arms, hauled her up on to her knees and held her in front of him in a firm grip.

The woman climbed on to the bed behind her. She was surprisingly agile for her age and terrifyingly at ease with the violent situation. The woman kneeled in front of Ylva, who was breathing heavily, her eyes darting everywhere.

'Look at me.'

Ylva looked up with uncertainty. Her hair was hanging

down in her face and the woman gently pushed it to the side and tucked it behind her ears.

'Stop panting.'

The woman spoke in a quiet voice, almost a whisper. Ylva gasped a few times more, the woman closed her eyes, smiled, and waited.

'Can we talk now?' the woman asked, so quietly that it was almost inaudible.

Ylva nodded weakly.

'Good.'

The woman looked at her husband, who let go of Ylva's arms.

'It's very simple,' she continued in a patient tone, almost like a teacher. 'You are here, and you know why.'

Ylva looked down.

'Look at me.'

Ylva lifted her eyes. The woman smiled at her, raised her eyebrows.

'You know why you are here.'

'I . . . '

The woman softly put her finger on Ylva's lips.

'Shh, no more about the past. You're going to pay back your debt. Let's look to the future now.'

The woman turned, sweeping out her arm.

'This is your world,' she said. 'You can use whatever is in this room. You might not think that it's much, that you might as well have nothing. But you're wrong. There's a lot that you take for granted, privileges you can't see.

The woman got down off the bed.

'I'll show you what we expect of you. When you hear us coming in, stand so that we can see you through the peephole. When we knock on the door, stand so that you are visible with your hands on your head, where we can see them. Do you understand?'

Ylva stared at her.

'You'll be given easy household chores such as laundry and ironing, but first and foremost you will always be available. My husband will use you whenever he feels like it, so that you never forget the reason why you are here. You will perform your tasks willingly and with conviction. There are various hygiene products in the bathroom and we expect you to use them. Do you understand?'

Ylva looked at the woman. The man was standing more or less behind her.

'You're crazy, both of you,' she said. 'Totally fucking insane. That was twenty years ago. Do you think Annika would be proud of you now? Do you think she'd feel she's been avenged?'

The woman slapped her hard across the face.

'I don't want to hear Annika's name pass your filthy lips.'

Ylva made an attempt to throw herself over the woman and wrestle her to the ground. The man came between them and twisted Ylva's arm up behind her back, forcing her to her knees. The woman hunkered down close to Ylva.

'If you try to escape again, my husband will dislocate your feet. So, in short, your life from now will be like *One Thousand and One Nights*. Minus all the tiresome stories. You will stay alive as long as it suits us.'

Someone called Karlsson from the police phoned just after eight on Monday morning. Mike replied that they still hadn't heard anything from Ylva and that he hadn't got any clues from anywhere else of where she might be.

Mike said with some irritation that he'd already spoken to the police about ten times on the Sunday. And on his own initiative had contacted the papers, who'd put in a notice under local news. Even though they hadn't mentioned Ylva by name or published a photograph.

'It's not necessarily as bad as you think,' Karlsson said. 'A couple of hundred people are reported missing every day in this country. Six to seven thousand a year. And only around a dozen or so of those disappear for ever. Generally due to drowning or something like that. My colleague, Gerda, and I were thinking about dropping by. Will you be at home for the next couple of hours?'

Gerda was, like Karlsson, a man. His surname was Gerdin, Karlsson explained, but as there weren't many women in the section, his colleagues had decided to rechristen him in the name of gender equality.

Mike's initial impression was that Gerda was the nicer of the two, only because Karlsson was the one who asked the questions. Both appeared to be incompetent, or, rather, resigned. As if they'd already decided that there was nothing they could do other than try to calm down hysterical family members and then wait and see.

'And you have a daughter together?' Karlsson asked.

'Sanna. My mother just took her to school.'

'Up there, in the yellow brick building?'

Karlsson pointed over his shoulder with his thumb.

'Laröd school, yes. Thought it was best if we kept things as normal as possible. I don't know what else to do.'

He looked at the policemen, hoping they'd agree. Gerda nodded and shifted his weight.

'How old is your daughter?' he asked.

'Sanna's seven. Turns eight in a fortnight. She's in Class Two.'

'Tell us in your own words what happened,' Karlsson said.

Mike sent him an irritated look. In his own words? Whose words would he use otherwise?

'She didn't come home,' he said. 'I collected Sanna from after-school club at about half past four. We went to the shops to buy food and then came home. Ylva had said that she might go out for a drink after work.'

'With her colleagues?'

'Yes, they were putting a magazine to bed and—'

'Putting to bed?'

'She works for an agency that produces company magazines. Putting a magazine to bed means they have to make the final changes before sending it off to print. It can take a while.'

'And did it?'

'No, not really. They were done just after six.'

'And you know that because . . .?'

'As I've already told several of your colleagues by now,

the first person I called was Nour, my wife's colleague and friend. She said that Ylva said goodbye to them on the street at quarter past six. Nour and the others went to a restaurant, Ylva said she was going home.'

Karlsson nodded thoughtfully.

'So, she said to you that she was going out for a drink with her colleagues, and she said to her colleagues that she was going home to you?'

'She said that she might go out for a drink with them. It wasn't decided.'

Karlsson cocked his head and he was bloody smiling too. Mike was close to thumping him.

'Look, I don't give a damn what you think. You want it to be something that it's not. Okay?'

Karlsson shrugged. 'I just thought it was a bit odd, to give out a double message like that. She says one thing to you, and something else to her colleagues. Don't you think that's a bit odd?'

'My wife has disappeared. She wasn't depressed, or suicidal, and to my knowledge has never been threatened in any way. And if she did happen to have a passionate lover stowed away somewhere, she'd at least phone her fucking daughter.'

'What makes you think she has a passionate lover?'

Mike glared at the policemen, from one to the other. Karlsson smiled at him.

'This is crazy,' Mike said. 'You're both crazy. Do you think it's funny? My wife has disappeared – don't you understand how serious that is?'

'We just wondered whether there was perhaps an explanation.'

25

The man and the woman took the mattress, the covers, the pillow and then turned off the electricity supply.

Ylva lay curled up on the floor with a towel over her body. She didn't know how long she lay there. She lay under the towel and cried, only getting up to drink and pee. When the power was finally switched on again, it was as if life had returned. The light on the ceiling came on and the TV screen flickered. It was daytime outside, afternoon, in fact, judging by the light and the lack of activity. The car wasn't in the driveway. Ylva wondered if Mike was managing to do the housework, what he was doing to find her. If he had followed her route home, put up posters with photographs of her. Had anyone seen her get in the car? She didn't think so.

What would she have done if she were Mike? Apart from all the obvious things like calling friends and the police and the hospital. She would put a notice in the paper, talk to any bus drivers who were working at that time. She would knock on every door between the bus stop and their house, ask if anyone had seen her passing, paper the town with photographs and missing person posters.

Then it struck her.

Mike might even knock on the door of the house where she was being held. He would introduce himself to the new couple and briefly explain what had happened. Then he'd show them a picture. The man and the woman would play interested, look closely at the picture, and then shake their heads in sympathy. The woman would put her hand to her heart and look distraught, the man would show concern and try to be helpful, suggest things, because men always do, seriously believing that they can solve all problems.

And Ylva wouldn't be able to make herself heard, she understood that now. Was there any other way she could attract attention?

Mrs Halonen was the first one to appear on the screen.

She went past with her Alsatian, turned into Bäckavägen. She glanced surreptitiously over at Ylva and Mike's house, almost guiltily. Ylva realised that she'd heard. And if Mrs Halonen knew, then everybody knew. She was way down the information chain.

Ylva tried to imagine the gossip, comforted herself with the conversations that were happening around town.

Did you hear that Ylva's disappeared?

Who?

Mike's wife, the girl from Stockholm.

What?

She didn't come home. Left work and never came home.

Has she run off?

Don't know.

She hasn't been in touch?

No, she's vanished. Mike's looking for her. He's reported it to the police and all that.

But I don't understand, she just didn't come home?

Nope.

But that's crazy. Has she left him?

I don't know.

What about the girl, she wouldn't just leave the girl, surely?

Either she's run away or something's happened.

Like what?

How should I know?

But she wasn't depressed, was she?

Things are not always as they seem. My dad had a friend who . . .

No matter what happened, things always blew over. Became part of life's great charade. Hundreds of passengers killed in a plane crash? Months later it would be forgotten, and only the anniversary would be marked. Thousands killed in a natural catastrophe? A week of grim news reports and then it turned into something you looked up on Wikipedia. The tsunami, what year was that? That's right, of course.

No one would save her, she had to escape.

Everyone went quiet when Mike entered Ylva's workplace. Nour got up and went over to meet him.

'Follow me,' she said. 'We'll go into the kitchen.'

Mike immediately started to cry. For the simple reason that a friendly person had seen his impotence and offered comfort.

'Fuzzy,' he said, when she asked how he was. 'It's like that protective plastic on new mobile phones or watches; if only someone could pull the bugger off, I'd see clearly.'

159

Nour nodded, wiped away a tear from his cheek with her thumb and handed him some water.

'Drink.'

Mike did as he was told, looked over her shoulder to check that the door was closed and waved his hand around nervously.

'Do you think she's met someone else?'

He looked at her with a mixture of fear and helplessness.

'Not that I know of,' she said, in the end.

'I don't see what else can have happened.' He shook his head and continued: 'She would have got in touch. She wouldn't just forget Sanna, would she?'

'No, she wouldn't,' Nour said.

'So what's happened then? Has she had an accident? Been run over, or met the wrong guy? I don't get it. Three nights, it's three nights now. I don't even know if I want her back, can you understand that?'

'I understand.'

Mike gulped down some air. Nour handed him a tissue and he blew his nose like a child, with no force.

'Mike, listen to me. You have to be strong. If nothing else, for Sanna's sake. She's a child, you're an adult. Do you hear what I'm saying, Mike? You're an adult.'

His telephone rang. Mike wiped his nose and looked at the display. He held it up for Nour to see and turned around.

'It's Mike,' he said.

'Karlsson here. I wondered if you could come by the station? There's something we'd like to show you.'

'Have you found her?'

'No, sorry. But we've got a list of the calls made to and from her phone. And a sound file of her voicemail.'

'I'm on my way.'

Mike hung up and turned to Nour.

'The police,' he said. 'They've got a list of her phone calls.'

Mike was nervous as he drove over. Tense and hopeful, frightened and resigned. He felt as if he was sitting a driving test. He parked outside the police station, just by the slip road to the motorway, and went in.

The woman at reception phoned Karlsson.

'They're expecting you,' she said, and smiled. 'Third floor, second door on the right.'

She could easily have been working in an advertising agency.

Karlsson was standing waiting in the corridor when Mike came out of the lift. He waved him over.

'Glad you could come,' he said, and led him into his office, where Gerda was already parked on a chair. 'Take a seat.'

Karlsson went round the desk to his computer.

'You said earlier that you called Nour first? Surely you must have tried your wife before then?'

'Of course.'

'And when did you call her the first time? Just so we know where it fits.' Karlsson pointed at the list in front of him.

'Don't remember,' Mike said. 'I thought about calling earlier to see if she was coming home for supper, but didn't.'

'Why not?'

'I didn't want her to feel guilty. I thought that she should be allowed to go out and enjoy herself on her own for a change.'

'So when did you call?'

Mike shrugged in exasperation.

'Before I went to bed,' he said. 'Around midnight?'

Gerda waved his hands around in the air, as if preparing himself to ask a difficult question, against his will.

'And, um, how do you get on, I mean, as man and wife?'

'Oh for Christ's sake, get real.'

162

Karlsson held up his hand in defence.

'Let's just listen to this,' he said, moving the mouse to the right sound file on the screen and clicking.

Mike heard his own voice and was struck by how feeble he sounded, subservient and uncertain.

Hi, it's me. Your husband. Just thought I'd see how you're getting on. I assume you're out with people from work. Anyway, I'm off to bed now. Take a taxi home, please. I've had a drink and can't drive. Sanna's in bed. Big hug.

Another, more mechanical, woman's voice said: *Received at zero zero fourteen.*

Karlsson stopped the recording and turned to Mike.

'First of all, do you usually introduce yourself as "your husband" when you call?'

'No, I was trying to be funny.'

'What do you mean?'

'I don't know.'

'Nor do I. But do you know what I think it sounds like? I think it sounds like you're really pissed off, but scared to show it. I think it sounds like a pathetic reminder. *You're not going to jump into bed with anyone else, are you? Remember that you're married. To me.*'

Mike stared at him. Karlsson didn't bat an eyelid. As if

he had just been declared the stupidest man in the universe and was proud of it.

Gerda flapped his hands around nervously.

'I wonder why you asked if she was out with people from work when you knew that's who she was out with. As if you thought she might be somewhere else.'

Just as bloody stupid.

'You sound nervous,' Karlsson continued. 'Are you?'

Mike looked at them.

'Is that the reason why you asked me to come?'

Karlsson pressed his fingers together under his chin. He reminded Mike of that executive guy on the old racist Mastermind box. The strategist, the thinker.

Karlsson leaned back and exchanged glances with Gerda. As if this was the piece of the puzzle they had expected to find. A soap opera of jealousy and passion that had gone off the rails.

Mike snorted with laughter. A cynical confirmation more than anything else.

'You'll have to excuse me,' he said. 'That's all you've come up with? That's the reason you asked me to come?'

Still no answer.

'Is this some kind of questioning technique, just sitting

there in silence? Do you actually suspect me, is that what it is? You think I've kidnapped my wife, or killed her and dumped the body? Is that it?'

'We just wondered if your wife had a lover.'

Gerda tried to make it sound trivial. Like a fact, like the colour of a house or the make of a car.

'No, my wife does not have a lover. She had an affair with a pretty awful bloke who, for obvious reasons, I don't have much time for. Let me put it this way, if Bill Åkerman disappears without a trace one day, I suggest you look me up and find out where I've been keeping myself. It was over a year ago and, no, I have no reason to believe that it's still going on. And in any case, Nour phoned him on Saturday, just to make sure. And no, Ylva wasn't with him.'

Mike stood up.

'If you'll excuse me,' he said, 'I think I'll go over the road to the newspaper and ask them to publish a photograph of my wife. Someone must have seen her. She can't just have vanished in a puff of smoke.'

26

'What was carried out with tremendous zeal? You're holding
back information.'

Jörgen Petersson sounded annoyed. Calle Collin sighed.

'You don't want to know,' he said.

'Of course I want to know,' Jörgen persisted.

'Believe me,' Calle said, 'you don't.'

'You're like one of those phoney conscientious news-
readers who warn viewers about disturbing pictures
knowing that's the best way to make people watch. You're
just trying to pique my interest, like a circus ringmaster
introducing a new act.'

'I've actually had problems sleeping.'

'Well, I've never had that problem. I sleep just like all the beautiful people in the adverts.'

Calle gave another deep sigh.

'Well, don't complain later then,' he said.

'Why would I complain?'

'I'm just saying.'

'I don't intend to complain.'

'Okay,' Calle said. 'Someone smashed Anders' head in with a hammer, pounded the hammer into his brain as if it were a butter churn, and then left the shaft standing up out of his skull like a dead flower in a pot.'

'Oh, fucking hell.'

'I told you, you didn't want to know.'

'Oh Jesus fucking Christ.'

'I don't want to hear you complaining.'

'And it was someone's better half who did it?'

'I think we can conclude that it was done by someone who wasn't very fond of our old classmate.'

'And the police think it was a man who committed the murder, but that it was a woman who lured him there?'

'More or less.'

'But they've got no idea who?'

'Not the faintest.'

Jörgen nodded silently to himself.

'So he was notorious . . .'

Calle started.

'What did you just say?'

'Anders Egerbladh,' Jörgen said. 'He must have been notorious.'

Calle looked at his friend long and hard.

'Have you been playing around?' he asked, finally.

'What are you talking about?'

'You said "notorious" – that's a dead giveaway, the code-word of someone who's been unfaithful. In order to play down their own excesses, they'll demonise others who are that little bit worse. It's like alcoholics who say they need a lager. Anyone who says "a lager" instead of "a drink" is by definition a serious alcoholic.'

Now it was Jörgen's turn to look at his friend long and hard.

'Now you've lost me.'

'Jesus, it's true,' Calle said.

'No, it's not,' Jörgen retorted. 'And no, I haven't been having a bit on the side.'

'I hope not,' Calle said. 'Because I like your wife more than I like you.'

'And if I should ever think about it, I wouldn't burden you with the knowledge.'

'I thank you for that.'

'Codeword,' Jörgen snorted. 'That's the most ridiculous thing I've heard.'

27

The restaurant had survived. Which was the most astounding thing. The lifespan of trendy, self-conscious cafés was normally short and the cycle was often the same: the place opened, the place was discovered, then the place was abandoned.

As a rule, the entrepreneur, intoxicated by the invasion, became ambitious and invested large sums in the hope of keeping his customers, but they swam in shoals that suddenly changed direction and disappeared without warning.

There were three reasons why Bill Åkerman's restaurant had survived. The first was that he had decided to stick with high-quality food and prices that bordered on indecent, despite an unexpected glowing write-up in the local paper. This made the restaurant an obvious choice for company dinners and people who didn't often go out but wanted to treat themselves once a year.

The second was its location. The restaurant was on the ground floor of an old villa just above Margaretaplatsen and had a panoramic view of the sound and the coast of Denmark.

The third reason was Bill's wife, Sofia.

Sofia managed the restaurant, employed people, came up with new menus, organised purchases and made sure that everyone was happy.

Bill knew that he couldn't have chosen a better partner. It was just a shame that she'd put on some extra pounds around the hips and, as a result, her self-confidence had plummeted and she had grown suspicious of his every move. But as she already knew about his affair with Ylva – and, like everyone else in Helsingborg, knew that Ylva was missing – Bill made no attempt to hide the fact that the police wanted to talk to him, as it actually reinforced the idea that Ylva was a cunning seductress who would leave any full-blooded man defenceless. Bill had already told them on the phone that he had no idea where Ylva was and had made it quite clear that he was no longer on intimate terms with her. But the police had insisted on speaking to him in person, all the same.

The meeting took place in the restaurant bar, which was empty despite the lunchtime rush.

'When did you last see Ylva?' Karlsson asked, having accepted a free coffee.

'Do you mean when did I last sleep with her or when did I last see her?'

'See her. And yes, sleep with her, too.'

'We had a brief affair in June last year. So that makes it, what, eleven months ago? The last time I saw her was on Kullagatan. I think it was in April, but I'm not entirely sure.'

'Did you talk to each other?'

'Yes. It was a bit awkward.'

'How do you mean?'

'It's not a big town, and there's always someone who's watching.'

'I see. And what did you say to each other?'

'Nothing in particular. She asked when we could start shagging again.'

That made Karlsson and Gerda sit up, they weren't sure whether he was kidding or not.

'That's what she said,' Bill assured them. 'And I told her: never.'

'Why not?'

'Because I don't want to. But I didn't say that. Spurn a woman, and you've got an enemy for life. You have to play it careful.'

'So what did you say?'

'I said that I didn't want to risk my marriage.'

'But that wasn't the real reason?'

'No.'

'So, why didn't you want to?'

Bill looked at them, shrugged.

'We like different things.'

The police officers were wide-eyed with dry throats, like two adolescent boys. Karlsson pulled himself together first.

'What do you mean, "different things"?' he spluttered, leaning forward with interest.

'She liked drama. She'd throw herself down, going, *Take me, take me* – that kind of thing.'

'I don't understand.'

'She wanted to be dominated.'

'You mean, tied up?' Karlsson asked, with the peeping-tom interest of a secret teenage masturbator.

'Not necessarily. But I don't think it's got anything to do with her disappearance. I'm just saying that she liked a bit of rough. Even though she looks so sweet. But that's sex for you. What's on the inside doesn't always match what's on the outside. Swings and roundabouts. The tough guy can be a gentle lover, skinny ones have more to prove.'

'What do you mean?' Gerda asked.

Bill Åkerman took a sip of coffee.

'She should have chosen a skinnier guy,' he said.

Karlsson threw the papers nonchalantly down on to the desk, pushed back his chair and stretched his legs.

'Okay,' he said and clasped his hands behind his neck. 'We've got a missing, horny away-player and a husband who's been cheated on. Conclusion?'

'She comes home late, it gets out of hand?' Gerda suggested.

'Yep,' Karlsson said and sighed. 'We'd better talk to the neighbours. They might have seen when she came home.'

'In the middle of the night?'

'Someone's always awake.'

'I thought we could talk to the girl,' Gerda said, and checked the time. 'She should be at school right now.'

'If we're lucky.' Karlsson nodded.

They parked behind the cafeteria and asked a passing pupil where the staffroom was. They were greeted by a large woman who had once been attractive and now tried to hide the fact that she wasn't any more. Karlsson and Gerda explained why they were there, and the woman knew immediately what it was about. Like the rest of the school staff, for the past couple of days she had talked of nothing but Ylva's disappearance. She asked Karlsson and Gerda to wait in the staffroom and went herself to fetch Sanna from her class.

When the woman came back, she was holding the girl's hand, apparently oblivious that the police could see how she cared for the children. The woman introduced Sanna to the policemen and said that they wanted to talk to her, maybe ask a few questions.

'It's nothing to be scared of,' she assured her, in her kindest child-friendly voice, and then turned to Karlsson and Gerda. 'Maybe it would be just as well if I stay?'

Karlsson nodded his consent and the woman sat down on the chair beside Sanna, without letting go of her hand.

'We've been talking to your dad,' Karlsson said, in the same voice that he always used, no matter who he was talking to. 'And he said that your mum's missing. Do you remember when you saw her last?'

Sanna nodded.

'When was that then?'

Sanna shrugged. Gerda gave it a try. He spoke in a softer voice than his colleague.

'Do you remember when you last saw your mummy?'

'Yes,' Sanna said.

'And where was that?'

'At school, here.'

The woman filled them in. 'Ylva dropped Sanna off at school on Friday morning. She spoke to the teachers. Mike was going to pick her up.'

Gerda gave a thoughtful nod and turned to Sanna again.

'And you haven't seen your mummy since then?'

Sanna shook her head.

'What did you and Daddy do at the weekend?'

'We went to Väla and McDonald's. And got out some films.'

'Sounds good.'

Sanna nodded. *The Parent Trap.*

Gerda didn't understand.

'It's really good,' Sanna said.

'Oh, I see, it's a film. Okay. Did Daddy watch it too?'

'He was talking on the phone.'

'When did he tell you that Mummy was missing?'

'When Granny came. Then the police.'

'Sanna, these gentlemen are also policemen.'

Sanna nodded obediently, but without much conviction.

'But the other ones were real policemen,' she said eventually. 'Daddy said that Mummy would come back when I was asleep, but she didn't. He said that she'd be back when I woke up. But she wasn't.'

Gerda sat on the edge of his chair and leaned forward towards Sanna, in an attempt to gain her confidence.

'And your mummy and daddy, do they argue a lot?'

Gerda stared out through the car window.

'I just hope it was him. If not, we've ruined his life. Mrs Mutton-Dressed-up-as-Lamb won't rest on her laurels.'

He was referring to the plump teacher who had sat in on the interview, savouring every word.

'You're the one who wanted to go there,' Karlsson said.

'So, conclusion,' Gerda said. 'Either she shows up with

her tail between her legs when she's finished screwing around, or he's killed her. There's no other option. And if he didn't do it himself, he hired someone.'

Karlsson chewed the skin at the side of his nail nervously.

'He could get us put away for something like this,' Karlsson said. 'And I'd report it, if it was me. Too bloody right, I would.'

'You know what?' Gerda said. 'He's got other things to think about.'

Karlsson turned on the radio. A presenter with an affected voice was talking unnecessarily fast and loud.

'Bloody talk radio,' he said, and switched it off again.

'It's all so strange, so hard to understand.'

Kristina had been sitting in front of the TV all evening. She'd seen what had happened and heard what was said, even though it had all gone over her head. She couldn't take any more of it. She blocked out the outside world.

A person couldn't just disappear?

A single thought occupied her mind, a single thought that prevented the TV images and sound from registering on her optic nerve or eardrums.

It was a thought that she mustn't think, didn't want to think – a horrid thought, which for that very reason refused to go away.

The thought that her son might have had something to do with Ylva's disappearance.

She couldn't get it to fit. She'd never known Mike to be violent. Quite the opposite; he was the quiet sort.

Had it been the last straw?

And if so, what did the future hold? Who would look after Sanna? Kristina imagined that everyone would keep their distance, too scared to get close. It would be hard for Sanna to find friends she could trust.

Kristina wanted to conjure up the image of some seriously disturbed psychiatric patient who might have stabbed her daughter-in-law to death on the street. She tried to imagine Ylva giggling irresponsibly in another man's bed, or laughing evilly. So that Mike would finally realise the kind of woman she was and free himself from her spell.

But none of these imagined scenarios succeeded in erasing the thought that she wanted to avoid at all costs. That Mike knew more than he was saying, that he'd had something to do with Ylva's disappearance.

Kristina heard the phone ringing. It had been ringing for

179

a while, but she hadn't counted the number of times. Finally her brain clicked into gear and she got up and went to answer it. She looked at the display and saw that it was Mike.

She took a deep breath, closed her eyes and said: 'Any news?'

Her son was crying on the other end.

'I've got no one to talk to,' he snivelled.

Kristina held her breath. She was prepared. For anything. It didn't matter. Mike was her son, nothing could change that.

'I'm listening,' she said. 'Carry on.'

She waited for him to pull himself together sufficiently that she could understand what he was saying.

'They went to the school,' he finally managed to squeeze out.

'Who?'

'The police. They talked to Sanna.'

Kristina didn't answer.

'Don't you understand?' Mike sobbed. 'They think it's me. They think I killed her. How can they even think that?'

His voice was helpless and desperate, but she couldn't hear any lies. Kristina felt the tension leave her muscles.

28

Karlsson and Gerda went from door to door and talked to the neighbours. Had anyone seen or heard anything that might shed light on Ylva's disappearance? Cars that had stopped nearby or left the Zetterbergs' house in the relevant time frame, which was probably between nine in the evening and the following morning.

Karlsson and Gerda were aware that every question they asked pointed suspicion in the same direction.

The result of two days' fieldwork was a couple of unconnected witnesses who had heard a car leave Bäckavägen and disappear up Sundsliden at around half past two in the morning. But unfortunately this lead came to nothing when it turned out that the car had been driven by a sober eighteen-year-old who had spent Friday evening round at his girlfriend's.

'Just our luck,' Karlsson said. 'Why couldn't he have stayed over? That's what we did in my day.'

'If I had a fifteen-year-old daughter, I wouldn't let an eighteen-year-old stay over, believe me,' Gerda retorted.

'No, I guess it's different if you've got girls. What d'you want?'

'Don't know.'

'Me neither.'

They were standing in a queue by an ice-cream kiosk.

'Maybe a soft ice,' Gerda said.

'Go for it.'

'With hundreds and thousands.'

'Hey big spender.'

'You only live once.'

'True. I think I'll go for three scoops. With strawberry sauce and cream.'

'So now you're going the whole hog?'

'Because I'm worth it. If you're going for hundreds and thousands, I'm having strawberry sauce and cream.'

They got their ice-creams and ate them leaning against the car in the sun.

'Doesn't get any better,' Karlsson said.

'Speak for yourself. My hundreds and thousands are finished.'

'Where would you dump the body?'

'Don't know. You?'

'In a lake,' Karlsson said. 'With weights.'

'Too much hassle,' Gerda concluded. 'You'd have to pull and drag the body around and have a boat. And then you'd be worrying that the body would decompose and float up to the surface. Bury the shit, I say.'

'But you'd have to dig bloody deep. There's always some animal that's rooting around in the dirt. God, it's so good when the cream kind of freezes on the ice cream and goes hard.'

'When it goes kind of lumpy, I know what you mean.'

'We'll have to talk to him again. It's been a few days now. Maybe his conscience has been doing its thing.'

Mike Zetterberg wondered what else he could do. He tried to think constructively, find a loose thread to pull at.

She hadn't been on the bus. Wrong, he didn't know for

sure. What he did know was that none of the bus drivers or passengers could remember seeing her. It was of course possible that no one had noticed her, but Mike found that hard to believe. Ylva attracted attention and had the sort of open smile that invited contact. She normally listened to her iPod so she wouldn't have to talk to people.

IPod in her ears? Could she have walked out into the road and been run over without anyone seeing it? And the driver had panicked and taken her lifeless body and buried it somewhere or thrown it into the sea. Not likely. She would have walked through the town, people everywhere. Extremely unlikely, almost impossible.

The most likely thing was, and he had to agree with the police here, that she had arranged to meet someone. She had said one thing to Mike and something else to her colleagues. To cover her back. The question was, who had she gone to meet?

Her phone records didn't provide any clues. He had gone through them himself with Karlsson and Gerda. Her emails at work were just as useless. No saved cyber flirts. She might of course have deleted them to avoid the risk of being discovered, or alternatively have a secret mail address, but Mike didn't think so. Middle-aged women who slept around were seen as liberated, they didn't need to skulk about. The opposite applied when you were a teenager: the girls got the bad reputation, the boys became heroes.

Ylva had been missing for four days. She hadn't just gone off for a dirty weekend with a hot lover. And her passport was still in the chest of drawers, so she hadn't taken a last-minute charter flight.

Her mobile . . .

Mike was just about to phone Karlsson and Gerda when he saw them turn into the driveway. He opened the front door and saw their serious faces.

'Have you found her?'

Karlsson put a hand on his shoulder.

'Let's talk inside.'

For the thirty seconds it took them to move into the kitchen and sit down, Mike was convinced that they'd found Ylva's body. It was a relief when he realised that she was still missing.

'Her mobile,' he said. 'Can't you see where she's been?'

'She turned her mobile off on Tågagatan.'

'When?'

'At half past six on Friday.'

'She should have been on the bus then,' Mike said.

'Why?'

'That's on the bus route, and it fits with when she left work.'

'But she wasn't on the bus,' Gerda stated.

'That's not why we're here,' Karlsson cut in. 'We've spoken to Bill Åkerman.'

Mike froze for a second.

'I see, and what did he say?'

'Well, first of all, he was working on Friday, the staff have confirmed that. But he told us something else that we thought was interesting.'

Mike leaned forward, all ears. Karlsson looked to Gerda for support.

'How was your sex life?'

Mike's face went bright red. But it was the red of anger, not embarrassment.

'What the fuck do you mean, *How was your sex life?* Our sex life *is* absolutely fine, thank you very much. The fact that she jumped into bed with that moron doesn't mean that she didn't love me, it's more that she doesn't love herself. Yes, I know how clichéd that sounds, but in her case it's actually true. My wife flirts, is always looking for pointless kicks. I've seen her dancing up tight with a neighbour several times, but I've also – and I assure you it's a thousand times worse – been forced to live with the anguish she feels afterwards, when she hates herself and just wants to die.'

'I thought you said she wasn't depressed.'

'Bill Åkerman was the final straw, the alarm bell she needed. It was like we started over again after that. And I'm sure that's one of the reasons she didn't go out with her colleagues.'

Karlsson and Gerda looked at each other and nodded.

Without a doubt.

29

It was difficult to hear what the other person was saying.

Calle Collin was sitting opposite an old actor, at a centrally positioned window table in an upmarket restaurant chosen by the actor. The other guests belonged to the same generation as the actor and glanced over at him discreetly. Two parties had passed the table on their way out and thanked the actor for many pleasurable moments and a lot of laughs. The actor had accepted these pats on the back with false modesty and great delight.

The reason that Calle Collin found it difficult to hear what the actor said was not that he spoke unclearly, but rather that he was so uninteresting.

'I . . . success . . . anecdote . . . pause for laughter . . . public record . . . troubled childhood . . . not so easy to succeed . . . all the same I . . . modest . . . I always doubt . . . I constantly fight . . . I . . . the main thing . . . I interpret . . . I get to the heart of the character . . . I . . . empty phrases . . . I.'

Calle Collin nodded attentively and wrote down key words. He felt melancholy. The actor wasn't a bad person, he was self-centred because he lacked self-confidence and therefore had an unquenchable need for confirmation. Moments like this were oxygen for him.

Calle Collin's interview would be a carbon copy of every other interview the actor had ever given. Nothing new would be added and the truth would be crystal clear in its absence. Calle would send the text over to the actor for approval and the actor would have his say and perhaps even hint that Calle's efforts didn't quite meet his expectations, as the promise of a page in a publication meant so much more to him now that he had long since passed the peak of his career.

Then the actor would delete the only thing that might be called a real observation on Calle's part and replace it with some self-glorifying statement, before both parties could agree that they were satisfied.

The actor had been interviewed countless times in the course of his career. The questions were always the same, as were the answers. Calle recognised the words that spewed out of his mouth from articles he had read before the interview. The words were exactly the same and so deeply entrenched that, even if the actor did want to open up and be honest, he couldn't possibly break free from the image he'd built up of himself.

'Why?' Calle blurted suddenly, without warning.

The actor was thrown off track in the middle of an anecdote that he'd told a hundred times before.

'Excuse me?'

Calle Collin realised that he'd been thinking out loud and didn't have a clue as to what the actor was actually talking about.

'How did you become who you became?' Calle tried, and changed his position.

'You should be who you are when you're not who you wanted to be,' the actor trotted out, well practised.

Calle gave him a friendly smile and nodded.

'Who were you at school then?' he asked. 'The class clown? A shrinking violet?'

The actor was silent for a long time before answering: 'I

was horrible,' he said, finally. 'I beat up others so they wouldn't beat me.'

Mike sat at the kitchen table. It was quiet, not even the fridge was humming. He thought about turning the page of the newspaper just to hear it rustle, but he knew that he wouldn't be able to lift his hand to make the movement.

He had done everything. That's certainly what he tried to tell himself. He didn't know whether it was true or not. Maybe he hadn't done anything. Maybe he'd just sat paralysed by the kitchen table with a newspaper in front of him that he hadn't read, a paper that he'd collected from the postbox, because he always collected the paper from the postbox. Every morning of his adult life.

Ylva hadn't come home and that was that. She'd gone to the office, spent the day there and then left work. But she hadn't come home.

Ylva had disappeared. She hadn't been in touch and she hadn't been seen. She was gone.

In five days' time, their daughter would turn eight. Sanna's classmates had been invited to the party. Mike didn't think that Ylva would come back for it.

Mike thought about their relationship, if it had been a relationship at all.

His mobile phone vibrated on the kitchen table and made a surprisingly loud noise in the silence. Mike looked at the display, saw that it was from the office and answered.

His colleague strained to be casual in a sympathetic way.

'Just wanted to check whether you'd be coming today.'

'Of course, I'm just on my way. I didn't sleep very well.'

'No rush,' the colleague assured him. 'The meeting's not until this afternoon.'

'Thanks for phoning,' Mike said.

He hung up and folded the newspaper. It was the tenth day since Ylva had disappeared.

30

People who claimed there was no difference between boys and girls had obviously never organised a children's party, Mike mused. The boys were boisterous and made a noise; they fought and spilled their popcorn and fizzy drinks, whereas the girls gathered round to watch Sanna open her presents.

How much of the difference was due to genetics or culture was another matter, but Mike was grateful that he had a daughter and not a son. Even though there were obviously exceptions. The kind, philosophical Ivan who, when asked how his mummy and daddy were, answered, *Not so good, in fact we're quite poor now, so we won't be able to go to Thailand.* Or the quiet Tobias who, a couple of years ago, had cried as though he'd never stop when he discovered that the party bags didn't include any chocolate buttons. Mike had made sure not to repeat the mistake at any birthday party since.

Mike and Kristina had carried an extra table into the kitchen so that there would be room for everyone. The table was set. Two other couples scooped ice-cream on to a serving plate full of meringues, Kristina sliced the bananas and Mike made up some jugs of squash. The noise and chaos in the sitting room was music to his ears, a reminder that life went on regardless, even though he himself was in a vacuum.

Because that's how it felt. Nothing changed, everything was the same. An ocean of words and stiff phrases uttered to make a point, to add importance, to gloss over and comfort. But they didn't prevent Holst from driving past in his Volvo estate or Mrs Halonen from waving in the distance as she passed with her Alsatian.

Life carried on. This inconceivable event was but a ripple on the surface, and would never be anything more. The sympathy from those around him had now boiled down to *Nothing new?* Which Mike answered with a troubled expression: Nothing new.

He looked at the clock. Twenty past two. The meringues were nearly ready. Judging by the noise level, it was like *Lord of the Flies* in the next room.

'Shall I go in and get them?' Mike asked.

'Yes, do,' his mother replied.

Mike went out into the sitting room, whistled loudly to shut them up and told them to come and get something to eat in the kitchen.

There were balloons tied to the postbox and the front door. Ylva watched the guests arrive on the screen. Sanna's class-mates were there, all dressed up and ready to hand over the wrapped presents. The children were welcomed into the house. Mike stood in the doorway and chatted with the parents.

Ylva thought they all looked uncomfortable, stiff and uncertain. She guessed that the fact that she was missing was still at the forefront of their minds. It would be strange if it wasn't.

The sun shone and the balloons danced and bobbed on the wind. Ylva realised that they wouldn't have been able to set the table with paper plates and plastic glasses outside. Anders and Ulrika stayed to help, and so did Björn and Grethe. Mike's mum had come over the evening before. The other parents were probably doing their own thing in the meantime: going for a walk, heading into town, to the cinema or something like that. If there was time. Parties normally didn't last more than two to three hours.

When all the guests had arrived and the door had been closed, Ylva couldn't see what was going on inside, but didn't find it hard to imagine. The noise from previous children's parties was still ringing in her ears.

For the next hour or so, nothing much happened other than Mike coming out with the rubbish. Then the terrace door was opened. The children spilled out in an organic mass. Mike and Anders divided them into teams and they did some kind of relay with oranges under their chins. Then they played hide and seek.

Mike and the other adults disappeared into the house. Fifteen minutes later, he stuck his head out of the door and shouted something. The kids stopped in their tracks and then rushed indoors.

Lucky dip, Ylva guessed.

The party would be over soon. The parents would be

back any minute now to rescue them from the noise and mess. Some would stay for a glass of wine in the kitchen and keep them company as they wound down and caught their breath after the timed chaos that was a children's party.

Sanna was buttering a piece of bread. She did this with such care that Mike and Ylva had started to put two knives in the butter before they put it on the table, one for them and one for Sanna.

Each slice was a work of art for Sanna that was not finished until the bread was covered in an even, smooth layer of butter. Without any bumps or marks.

'So, do you think it was a good party?' Mike asked.

Sanna nodded without lifting her eyes from the bread.

This fixation with spreading the butter was a running joke for Mike and Ylva. They wondered what it might indicate, speculated where she might have got it from and what other things in life would be given such time and care.

At times, Ylva worried that Sanna might have some kind of disorder, a touch of autism or some condition known by an acronym. But that wasn't the case. Mike guessed that spreading butter was a form of meditation. And there was absolutely no point in analysing to death something that worked. A lot simpler to put an extra knife in the butter. Live and let live. With all our individual peculiarities.

'What was most fun?' Mike wondered.

'Mummy's not coming home, is she?'

The question was like a slap in the face. Mike had thought a great deal about his mother's misguided decision, keeping his father's suicide secret from him and talking evasively of a car crash. He recalled how the feeling of hopelessness and guilt had floored him when the truth finally came out. Mike had decided not to embellish or protect his daughter from the truth.

'No,' he said, 'it doesn't look like it.'

Sanna looked at him.

'Is she dead?'

'I don't know,' Mike replied. 'I don't know anything.'

Sanna put the knife back in the butter and started to eat. She glanced quickly down at the table before looking out the window to the world beyond: light green leaves, flowering lilac, it would be the summer holidays soon.

Mike's eyes filled and his nose got blocked, forcing him to breathe through his mouth.

31

Friendliness, privileges

When the victim has been sufficiently broken in, the manipulation becomes even more devious. The perpetrator, who has hitherto physically abused and mocked the victim, is suddenly kind and generous. The victim becomes confused and starts to reassess the perpetrator, to the point of denying earlier assaults. The perpetrator was only doing what he had to. The victim understands him. The victim starts to experience her situation as normal and self-inflicted.

'Close your eyes.'

Ylva looked at him warily. She was standing with her

hands on her head, as she'd been instructed to do. He had opened the door just enough to peer round it.

'It's a surprise,' he said. 'Close your eyes.'

She obeyed, her eyelids quivering uneasily. She heard him come in through the door and walk towards her. She opened her eyes. He was holding a floor lamp in one hand and a heavy paper bag in the other.

'Something to read,' he said. 'It's nice to have something to pass the time. Do you use glasses?'

She shook her head. The man smiled at her.

'Sit down,' he said.

Ylva did as she was told. The man put the bag and the lamp on the floor, and sat beside her on the bed.

'You're here now,' he said. 'I know that it's hard to accept. You want to think that it's temporary, that you'll be able to get away. Even though you know that will never happen. And the sooner you stop thinking that, the sooner you'll settle down. Believe me, in a year's time you won't want to leave. In a year's time, you'll stay, even though I open the door.'

He stroked her hair. As if she was a child and he was comforting her, the wise adult.

'And it's not a bad life, the one we can give you,' he said.

He put his finger under her chin and turned her face gently towards him.

'Violence isn't really my thing,' he said. 'I only hit you because I have to, to make you obey. It's effective, but doesn't help build strong bonds. I prefer the carrot to the whip, praise to censure ... '

'But what do you want us to do?'

Like most men, Karlsson was in fact soft. The unshaven and red-eyed husband of a missing wife was more than he could cope with. If Karlsson hadn't been convinced that Mike's tears were due to guilt rather than grief, he could have got him to do anything.

'I want you to find her,' Mike said.

'How?' Karlsson asked.

Mike didn't know.

'Either she doesn't want to be found, or ... '

Karlsson stopped himself, but it was too late. Mike was crying again.

Good God, what a pansy, Karlsson thought. If he doesn't stop the waterworks soon, he'll get me started too.

'Sorry,' Mike sobbed.

'Not at all,' Karlsson said. 'Perfectly understandable.'

He opened his drawer and found a packet of tissues that he pushed across the table.

'Thank you,' Mike said.

Rusty knife, Karlsson thought.

Crime of passion, rusty knife, guilt.

32

A foreign country was always a good place to hide your alco-
holism. The man assumed that was why all Western men
living in exile were so confusingly alike.

Johan Lind was, to be fair, married to an African woman
and the proud father of two small children, but the whites
of his eyes were bloodshot and jaundiced, his cheeks were
puffy and his stomach was tight as a beer barrel, like most
white men in the Third World.

Johan Lind started to drink at lunchtime and often
stopped by a bar on his way home from work. The bar was
a corrugated-iron shack that offered only the local beer and

a handful of young women who sat on men's knees and laughed at their jokes, in return for drinks and tips.

The man guessed that this was how Johan Lind would justify his wayward life. Something evasive like them being poor in Africa, but at least they know how to have fun. Everything wasn't so damn serious. People had forgotten how to laugh in Sweden.

Something along those lines.

The man couldn't be certain that Johan Lind was actually of that opinion, as he kept his distance and made his observations from a rental car, but it seemed a qualified guess.

The man had been in Zimbabwe for six days now and wanted to accomplish what he had set out to do as soon as possible. He had learned the following: Johan Lind worked as a foreman on a construction site in central Harare. He lived with his family in Avondale, a nice suburb to the northwest of the city. Every working day was the same.

The man was waiting for the right moment. Which came the next day.

Johan Lind had decided that, as it was Friday, he would take his motorbike to work. It was a mean machine with high suspension and erratic acceleration. The man saw him pull out from his house and speed up on the bend as if he was still a death-defying twenty-something-year-old.

More than just a bit pathetic, the man thought, as he followed him at a distance to his workplace in town.

When Johan Lind, true to habit, stopped at the bar on the way home from work, the man decided it was time.

He waited further down the road. When Johan Lind drove past a few hours later at a more leisurely pace than normal, his speed reduced slightly to compensate for his alcohol consumption, the man turned the key in the ignition of his rental car and pulled out after him.

It was dark and there weren't many cars around.

The man held back until they came to a stretch of road without houses. Then he overtook and swung the car across the road in front of the motorbike. Johan Lind lost control and toppled over. The bike spun away from him and he lay there on the asphalt. The man parked up by the side of the road and hurried back to him.

'You idiot – you fucking drove me off the road!' Johan screamed.

The man went up to him, looked hastily around. Johan Lind tried to blink away the pain.

'Are you all right?' the man asked.

Johan Lind was startled when he heard his mother tongue. He looked up in surprise at the reckless driver who had so nearly cost him his life. He seemed familiar.

'Let me help you,' the man said. 'I'm a doctor.'

He placed his arm under Johan's neck and took a firm grip.

'Do you remember Annika?' he said, and then broke his fellow countryman's neck.

'In other words, you've got nothing?'

The public prosecutor glanced up from the papers he had demonstratively continued to read while Karlsson and Gerda rattled through the information they had gathered in connection with Ylva Zetterberg's disappearance three months earlier.

They had concentrated on the missing woman's affair, her conflicting messages about where she was going that Friday evening and, finally, her alleged liking for a bit of rough in the sack.

Karlsson and Gerda looked at one another, each hoping that the other would come up with a neat paraphrase that would lend authority to the thin and, in practice, useless report.

The public prosecutor continued to sort his papers, a clear indication of how little he valued their work.

'No body, no witnesses, no inexplicable bank withdrawals, no mysterious emails or phone calls – in short, nothing.'

He looked at them for a response. Neither Karlsson nor Gerda said anything.

'Then the case is closed,' the public prosecutor said, and returned to his papers without paying any more attention to the two policemen.

'That is all,' he added in a quiet voice.

33

There was such a thing as the professional mourner, someone who went to funerals where they had no reason to be, who cocked their head and nodded sympathetically with a pained expression. They turned out in numbers. But most people withdrew. The vast majority were nonplussed by other people's grief, they didn't know what to do or say. They were afraid of being intrusive, of being a reminder and adding to the pain. They were also frightened that some of the heaviness and sadness might spill into their own lives.

Those who had experienced grief and loss and had been

confronted with the uncertainty of those around them often said afterwards that it didn't matter so much how those around them responded, what was important was that they did. In whatever form that took.

In Mike's case, there was nothing to grieve, only uncertainty and questions.

'And she's just disappeared?'

'Yes.'

'So, she's run off?'

'No, I don't think so.'

'Did something happen then?'

'I don't know. She's missing. She left work and never came home.'

'What do the police say?'

'Nothing really. They said that it happens, people just disappear.'

'She must be somewhere. I don't understand . . .'

Mike's friends and colleagues couldn't offer their condolences. To do so would signal that they'd given up hope. After a while, they started to keep their distance. There was nothing more to say. Ylva's disappearance was a mystery.

When she'd been gone five months, the local paper did a long article in conjunction with the TV programme,

Missing, in an attempt to bring to light more information. The article detailed Ylva's last day at work. It also included a list of those who had disappeared without trace in the region in recent years, under the heading *People whose bodies have never been found*.

Most of them were men, more than half of whom were feared lost at sea. Some of them had been seen in the days after they'd disappeared, but the witness reports were conflicting and vague.

In his capacity as investigating officer, Karlsson made statements, rattling off statistics and possible scenarios.

'In cases where we suspect that the missing person may have been killed, we concentrate on those closest to them. That's usually where we find the culprit.'

The statement didn't name Mike directly, but the article was illustrated with a photograph of Ylva, which the paper had been allowed to borrow in connection with her disappearance.

Karlsson couldn't have pointed his finger more clearly, without the risk of libel.

Mike spent the greater part of the following week refuting the accusations.

He phoned Karlsson, who claimed that he had been

misquoted and misunderstood. He had been talking in general terms and not specifically about Ylva's disappearance.

The public prosecutor said that it was a matter for the Swedish Press Council.

'And if you read it correctly, then—'

Mike threw down the phone and called the newspaper.

'My daughter was crying when I picked her up from school today. And guess what the other children had said?'

The managing editor was apologetic and understanding and said he was willing to publish a correction, which he did. A small notice on the front page, which stated that neither the police nor the public prosecution authority had named any suspects from Ylva's closest family and friends.

As with most denials, this just made matters worse.

34

Ylva lay in bed looking at the TV screen. The light was taking over, morning forcing back the night. It was the best time of day. She knew that she would soon see Sanna and Mike flit past the windows and three-quarters of an hour later leave the house and get into the car.

Ylva stared at the screen as if their safety depended on her vigilant supervision. She concentrated so hard that everything around her disappeared. It was almost as if she was there, inside the image of reality that she was watching.

Mike and Sanna had found new routines. It was obvious from their familiar movements. The way Mike closed the front door, the way Sanna walked round the car and jumped in as soon as he opened it. The booster was now a permanent fixture on the passenger seat. Sanna put her backpack down under the seat and reached up for the safety belt. Mike might throw out yesterday's rubbish. Hesitate for a moment before he emptied the right things into the right bins.

Mike had adapted his working day to suit Sanna's timetable. In the mornings, at least. His mother was there most afternoons. She came back hand in hand with Sanna from school, carrying bags of food.

Ylva wondered whether her mother-in-law was happy now. If she truly valued the importance she had acquired.

Kristina had also lost a spouse. The difference was that she'd known. She had almost certainly taken her fair share of the blame, gone over and over what she might have done differently, punished herself in that way. But she had known.

Sanna had a new autumn jacket. Ylva was sure that Mike had let her choose it herself. She thought to herself that she wouldn't have been so generous.

As soon as they had disappeared from the screen, Ylva started her morning exercises. Five minutes marching on the spot, pulling her knees up high, hands at her side. A hundred sit-ups and twenty-five push-ups.

Ylva wanted to do more, but was afraid that she might injure herself and have to stop altogether. The feeling of strength was important to her mental wellbeing.

They had murdered Anders, they had murdered Johan. Murdered. The man had told her proudly, in great detail, and informed her what they now expected from her.

There was no rush, the woman had explained. Ylva could prolong her own suffering if she liked, she didn't deserve a quick fix. But when she was ready, they would provide her with the necessary equipment.

Then the woman had complained about the smell of sweat. She complained about everything. Ylva was more scared of her than of the man.

Once she had showered, Ylva made a cup of tea and buttered a slice of bread. Then she did the laundry and ironing, the jobs she had been given. She carried them out with surprising energy and care. She was given food, electricity and water in return for her work. Allowed to carry on living.

The floor lamp, electric kettle and books were in return for the other thing.

Ylva deserved rewards, she did more than was expected of her.

And she was always ready.

Calle Collin was in the Odengaten branch of Stockholm Public Library. There were signs everywhere that said that you could only take one newspaper at a time, but Calle was in a hurry and so grabbed half a dozen of the local newspapers before he sat down in the reading room.

Journalism was cyclical. The one thing spawned the next, which in turn required research, which resulted in new articles, which spawned . . . etc.

Textbooks tended to emphasise the importance of multiple, independent sources. Access to objective information was a prerequisite for good citizens to make considered choices and then vote for the party that he or she believed was best placed to rule the country for the coming parliamentary term.

Political journalism was not really Calle's bag. His 'cause' was primarily to keep the wolf and creditors from his door, but even the content of the weeklies worked on the same cyclical basis. He got ideas for his own material from other people's articles.

He flicked through the papers quickly, looking for material with a trained eye. The notices in local papers were what interested him. That was where he normally found stuff, unusual events in normal people's lives.

He made a quick note of everything that caught his eye. Even if it wasn't suitable for an article or interview, it could perhaps be turned into a Readers' Own Story. These weren't as well paid, but easy to cobble together. Calle had been working as a freelancer for a family magazine for a while now, providing that sort of copy, and had soon come to realise that it was far simpler to write the article yourself than to edit the incomprehensible manuscripts that readers sent in.

Thirty minutes later, Calle left the library. He went home and fired off emails with ideas for three stories to four editorial desks. To send any more suggestions would test the patience of the editors.

He would call them in the afternoon and ask if they'd managed to look at his suggestions. Hopefully, some of them would be cautiously positive.

He heard the post drop through the letterbox – the postman must have been a basketball player in the past. Calle went out into the hall and picked up the window envelopes with a sigh. He opened them with his thumb and, true to form, confirmed that even when things looked bad, they could always get worse.

Three hours later he had spoken to the fourth and final features editor. No takers. Two of them said they would think about a couple of the ideas but couldn't promise anything. One had been openly disinterested and sighed loudly when Calle introduced himself. Another, a young man with great social skills but obviously very little between the ears, had declined and wittered on about cutbacks. Calle was sure that the guy would swiftly clamber his way to the top of Sweden's largest media group.

Calle had just laid down on the bed and started to stare at the ceiling with apathy when the phone rang. He checked the display. Helen, the managing editor of *Children & Family*. Calle answered brightly.

'It's been a while.'

'Yes,' she said, harassed. 'And I'm sorry. We've had so much to do. And still do. Which is why I'm calling. Quick question. Could you come in and do some editing?'

'Absolutely. When?'

'Tomorrow and Friday. And the whole of next week.'

'Of course,' Calle said.

'Really? That's fantastic. I love you.'

'No problem,' Calle said, and hung up.

'The phone just hasn't stopped ringing,' he said out loud, with a huge grin.

35

Ylva was dead, Mike was certain of it. He no longer held out any hope that she would suddenly get in touch from somewhere on the Mediterranean, where she was picking grapes in sandals and loose clothing, making trouble as a horny, post-pubescent hippie. Something had happened and he didn't care to speculate too much about what. Instead of ruminating on how terrifying the final hours of her life might have been, Mike consciously blocked all thoughts that led in this direction and focused instead on the practicalities of what lay ahead.

'Daddy, you've been invited to a fancy dress party!'

'What, have I?'

Sanna came running towards him with the invitation in her hand. Mike lifted his daughter up and hugged her tight. He nodded to his mother, who was standing in the kitchen in her apron, smiling as she looked on.

'What are you going to wear?' Sanna squealed.

'I don't know. Let's have a look at the invite.'

He put Sanna down and took the card that she handed him. He hung his jacket up and was reading as he walked into the kitchen.

'So, she's turning forty,' he said, and kissed his mother on the cheek. 'Mmm, smells good.'

'It's just meatballs, nothing special.'

'Couldn't be any more special.'

'What are you going to go as?' Sanna nagged.

'I don't know. Let's see if I go, first of all.'

'What? Aren't you going to go?'

This was beyond Sanna's comprehension. A fancy dress party, the chance to dress up. The best of the best.

'Of course Daddy's going to go,' Kristina said.

'We'll see,' Mike remarked, and sneaked a meatball straight from the pan.

Sanna looked at her father in disappointment.

'You never want to do anything fun.'

'Don't I?' Mike asked.

'No, never,' Sanna said.

'But maybe I don't think fancy dress parties are that great.'

'Daddy, you don't think anything's great.'

Calle Collin gave a loud sigh. The article was nonsense and bore no relation whatsoever to the heading. The quotes were inane, the facts nothing new and the angle about as exciting as a night out in Nässjö.

It was Friday afternoon and the editorial team for *Children & Family* were sitting in the kitchen drinking coffee. Helen had tried to get Calle to join them, but he refused to leave his desk until the article was set. It was his last day as an editorial temp and he wanted to get it finished, even if he couldn't for the life of him understand why Helen had bought the story in the first place.

The phones kept ringing all around him, first one, then the other.

'Could you ring reception and ask them to hold all calls?' Helen shouted through. 'Say that we're in a meeting until four.'

Calle picked up the phone and dialled.

'I think it might be best if you took this call all the same,' the switchboard operator said. 'I actually think Helen should take it herself.'

'Okay, transfer it then.'

Calle introduced himself to the woman, who was extremely distressed and demanded to talk to the managing editor.

'What's it concerning?' Calle asked, as he didn't want to disturb the team's coffee break for yet another subscriber who hadn't got their magazine on time.

It took about half a minute before Calle realised that this was serious.

'Just a moment,' he said. 'I'll go and get her.'

He put the receiver down on the desk, swallowed an uncomfortable lump in his throat and went out to the kitchen. The expression on his face obviously reflected what was going on in his head, because everyone fell silent and looked at him in suspense.

'There's a woman on the phone,' Calle said. 'Something about a report in the last edition. About Africa.'

Helen nodded.

'Yes. What about it?'

'The guy's dead,' Calle said. 'He was killed in a road accident four months ago.'

'Oh dear God.'

Helen got up quickly.

'Your phone?' she asked.

Calle nodded.

He stayed in the kitchen and, like the others, listened to Helen's measured and calm response. Her concern and sincere apologies, her deepest sympathies. And, given the situation, her honest but meaningless explanations for the mishap.

One of the reporters had managed to find a copy of the relevant edition and turned to the article in question. Though it had been written six months ago, it had not been used until now. Calle leaned over the table to get a look at the man who had died in a road accident four months ago. The man was posing proudly with his family, an African wife and two children. A baby girl, judging by the clothes, and a son of about two.

It took a few moments for Calle to recognise him. He felt his heart beat faster as he searched for the man's name in the text. He was right. It was him.

The man who had been killed in an accident in Africa

was Johan Lind, one of the playground tyrants who was part of what Jörgen Petersson had called the Gang of Four.

Mike did go, even though he viewed fancy dress parties as a crime against human dignity, something that only dull, unimaginative and sadistic people would come up with.

He went for Sanna's sake. To be a good example and not someone who said no to life.

Virginia was the formal type, with pursed lips and an unsympathetic face, cold and distant. Virginia was also, after half a glass, a crazy party animal.

And on those occasions, Mike thought about as much of Virginia as he did of fancy dress parties.

The other guests patted him on the shoulder and said that it was good to see he was getting out again.

It was now ten months since Ylva had disappeared and nearly six months since the newspaper article. Mike's breathing was shallow, as if he was about to start crying. It had become a habit, the way he breathed.

The dinner was pleasant enough. Virginia was true to form, Dr Jekyll and Mrs Hyde.

It was later, once the table had been cleared and the music was thumping with youthful imprudence and playful erotic thrusts, that Virginia pulled him over and screamed in his ear: 'I think you know.'

She nodded drunkenly and jabbed her finger at Mike's chest. He had a horrible premonition, but it was so unthinkable that he couldn't bear to acknowledge it.

'Know what?'

'What?'

She was really drunk.

'Know what?' Mike repeated in a loud voice.

Virginia stumbled forward and waved at Mike to bend down so she could shriek in his ear.

'Ylva,' she screamed. 'I think you know what happened.'

Mike stared at her with his mouth open and a quickening pulse. She gave an alcohol-infused shrug and pointed at everyone around.

'They all do.'

36

Mike sat up half the night with his mother and didn't manage to sleep for many of the few hours that remained. When he had stared long enough at the light that seeped in through the bedroom curtains, he pulled on a pair of jeans and a T-shirt and went over to Tennisvägen to see Virginia and her husband. It was nine o'clock and they had just got up.

Lennart opened the door. Mike marched past him into the kitchen where Virginia tried to hide her embarrassment behind the newspaper and claimed that she couldn't remember anything.

'Don't give me that crap,' Mike said, pointing an accusing finger at her. 'Don't give me that fucking crap. Ylva's missing, presumably dead, and you think it's funny to lay that shit on me. Something to gossip about over a glass of wine.'

Lennart took a step forward, tried to play the man.

'Mike, why don't you sit down, then we can talk this through sensibly?'

'Don't touch me.'

Mike's breathing was audible.

'I was so pleased to get your invitation,' he said. 'And then you throw that shit in my face.'

Virginia sat in silence, her cheeks burning red.

'What the hell were you thinking? Do you think, do you both seriously think that I've got something to do with Ylva's disappearance? Do you really?'

'Of course we don't,' Lennart assured him. 'It was a misunderstanding. Wasn't it, Virginia?'

She sat paralysed, didn't move a muscle.

'Well, let me tell you that I had absolutely nothing to do with Ylva's disappearance. She has been missing for ten months and seven days. And not an hour passes without me wondering what happened the night she disappeared, not a single hour. I just hope it was quick, that she didn't suffer.

And you have the gall to sit here and presume you know. To speculate! You should be fucking ashamed of yourselves, both of you.'

Mike turned to face Lennart, stared at him with contempt.

'Riding around on your Harley without a silencer, do you know that everyone's laughing at you? A middle-aged man on a motorbike. What next? An electric guitar? If you had any idea of what I've gone through, what Sanna and I have to face every day, you wouldn't say that sort of thing, you miserable bastards.'

Virginia sat there without saying a thing and stared at the table. Lennart made another attempt to get the upper hand.

'Mike, for Christ's sake.'

'Just shut up. You haven't got the balls.'

Mike slammed the door behind him. He ran up the steps to Ankerliden and carried on towards Bäckavägen. He walked fast, even though it was a steep slope, and felt more confident in his step and calmer in his heart than he had done for a long time.

When he got home, his mother and Sanna were up and breakfast was on the table.

His daughter looked at him.

'Where have you been?'

'I went down to see Virginia and Lennart. There was something I had to say to them.'

'Was the fancy dress party fun?'

Mike stretched out his arms and lifted her up.

'It was great fun,' he said and spun round in a jig.

He held Sanna tight and smiled at his mother.

Mike dropped Sanna off at school and drove straight to the hospital. He paid for a full day in the car park. He had no idea how long it would take but assumed that it might take a while.

He walked over to the lifts and read the sign. Fourth floor.

The door into the corridor was locked, so Mike pressed on the bell. A nurse appeared and walked towards him with raised eyebrows and a question mark on her face. He was wearing an expensive suit and obviously didn't look like a patient.

She opened the door.

'How can I help you?'

'My wife is missing, presumably dead. My neighbours

think I'm behind it. I have a daughter who is eight, I need help. Someone to talk to.'

He saw the nurse hesitate, as if she thought it was maybe a joke. Then she gave a quick nod.

'Have you been here before?'

Mike shook his head.

'Follow me,' the nurse said.

She showed him where to wait and promised to be back shortly.

It only took a couple of minutes. She returned with the doctor, a man of around sixty. Mike thought he looked familiar. Maybe a parent of one of his friends.

The man held out his hand. Mike shook it, gratefully.

'Hello. My name is Gösta Lundin. You want to talk to someone?'

Mike nodded.

They went into one of the rooms and the doctor closed the door behind them.

'Please, sit down.'

'Thank you.'

Gösta Lundin sat down on the other side of the desk.

'I'm sorry, but I didn't catch your name.'

'Mike, Mike Zetterberg.'

The doctor started, looked up at him briefly and then wrote down his name.

'ID number?'

Mike rattled off his number.

The doctor placed his pen on the desk and smiled at Mike.

'Good,' he said. 'So, you just came here without an appointment?'

'Yes.'

'And why was that?'

Mike told him the story.

'. . . she just never came home,' he concluded. 'It was no more dramatic than that. I have no idea what's happened to her, whether she had an accident or was murdered.'

'But you think that she's dead?'

There was a pause before Mike answered. He wanted to be sure of his words.

'I find it difficult to believe anything else.'

'You said that your friends suspect that you might have something to do with your wife's disappearance. Do the police share this view?'

'My wife had an affair a year or so before she disappeared. And, for all I know, maybe not just the one. When

I told them that, the officers leaned back and looked at each other. As if they were just waiting to ask where I'd hidden the body.'

'But that didn't upset you as much?'

'It was upsetting and offensive in every way, but at the time, in the chaos that followed my wife's disappearance, I basically couldn't have cared less. There was no official charge, more insinuations in the form of exchanged looks and silent observation. As if they were waiting for my conscience to get the better of me and for me then to break down and tell them what I'd done.'

'So why is it different now?'

'Because I've just managed to settle back into what we call everyday life. The party felt like a turning point. It was a fancy dress party. I hate dressing up. But I went, just to prove that I was back on track.'

Mike looked up. Met the doctor's gimlet eyes.

'You think that it shouldn't bother me?' he said. 'What the neighbours think and do. That, given everything else, it shouldn't make a difference?'

Gösta Lundin shook his head, without taking offence.

'I didn't say that. And it wasn't what I meant either.'

Mike regretted saying what he had.

'I'm sorry.'

'Not at all. I just want you to say how you feel. And what about the sense of loss?'

'Like a hole, I'm just a shell and there's an echo inside. That's how it feels. Though sometimes I wonder if I really do feel that or if that's just how I am expected to feel. Sometimes it's like sweat on your forehead. There's a pressure and dull thumping inside your skull. Not metallic, more . . . I don't know, muffled. It's physical, put it that way. But more often there's a kind of distance.'

'Kind of distance? What do you mean?'

'People's voices. It's as if I'm disconnected. I hear them, but I'm wandering around in my own fog, almost like I'm drunk. But not, at the same time. It's more that I see myself as another person, as though I'm standing outside myself. When I hold out my hand and take someone else's, it's as if I've got nothing to do with me. The same when I'm talking: it's not me. The words come out of my mouth like a foreign advert that's been badly dubbed, my mouth doesn't synch with the sound. But even more, it's as if nothing's changed. Everything is just the way it was before, everything just carries on.'

'Your daughter,' the doctor probed.

'Sanna ...' Mike said. 'I don't know. It feels like she's moved on, done her grieving, accepted. Yes, that's it. Mummy was there and now she's not. Doesn't exist any more. It's almost frightening.'

'Is she happy?'

'You mean, in general? Yes, I think so. No, I know she is. Every day is an adventure.'

'Has she got friends?'

'Oh yes.'

'So, what you're talking about, what you suspect, none of it has spilled over on to your daughter?'

'No, if it had, I'd go mad.'

Gösta Lundin moved on his chair.

'So, really, what we're talking about is something that a drunk and not particularly intelligent woman came out with at a party?'

Mike snorted with laughter. Gösta looked at him intently. Mike shook his head.

'Did you know that you have to wait five years before someone can be declared dead?' he asked. 'And then it's the tax authorities who announce it first, while you still have to wait another six months. But what then? Do you invite people to a funeral and sit there and look at an empty coffin and talk about a person no one remembers any more? And why the tax authorities? What have they got to do with it?'

'You confronted the woman,' Gösta said. 'Tell me about that.'

'I went to her house. At first she claimed that she couldn't remember anything, then her husband said that I'd misunderstood her. She was obviously embarrassed.'

'But you're convinced that she said what everyone else is thinking?'

Mike nodded.

'And if you follow that thought through to its conclusion? Imagine that it's all your friends and acquaintances talk about, nothing else. Constantly. That they sit around in groups and nod in agreement with every accusation that is voiced or insinuated.'

Mike looked at the doctor, who was smiling at him.

'Then you realise how ridiculous it is, don't you?'

'Yes, maybe.'

'I think it's a good thing that you came here. I suggest that we make another appointment straight away and that we continue to meet regularly until things get easier. Is that okay with you?'

Mike nodded gratefully. Gösta Lundin looked up at him as he leafed through his diary.

'You look familiar,' he said. 'I think I may have seen you in Laröd. Do you perhaps live there?'

'Hittarp,' Mike said. 'Gröntevägen.'

'Gröntevägen,' Gösta repeated. 'That's what I thought. My wife and I have just moved here from Stockholm. We live some way up Sundsliden.'

Mike looked surprised.

'Really? And we haven't met?'

'I think I've seen you,' Gösta said. 'But you've had other things on your mind, for obvious reasons.'

'But all the same,' Mike said. 'We're practically neighbours. You mean the white house on the hill? The one that was renovated? With a music studio in the basement?'

Gösta put down the diary and strummed an air guitar while he hummed the intro to 'Smoke on the Water'.

Mike couldn't hold back the laughter. A psychiatrist pretending to be a pop star – the unexpected simplicity was beautiful.

'Though it's mainly drums,' Gösta said. 'That's my release. Bang, hit, bang, hit. Let go of all the rubbish.'

37

It was important to show feeling, to respond convincingly. Ylva performed her only duty well, she was convincing. It wasn't hard, she almost looked forward to the visits. Any form of human contact was preferable to the isolation and loneliness. What they had told her was true, she had learned to be content with what she had.

Ylva alternated in her role as mistress, from vampish and challenging to timid and innocent.

It was unbelievably embarrassing. He was over sixty, educated and intelligent, and should know better. But Gösta Lundin was no different from other men. He chose to believe in her lusty moans, chose to believe that she arched her back to increase her ecstasy, chose to believe that she pulled him close to be filled with his manhood.

When he knocked, she stood in front of the door where she could be seen, with her hands on her head. She stood like this until he had come into the room and looked to check that the knives, scissors, iron and kettle were in place on the worktop. All these items were potential weapons and if he couldn't see them, he would hit her, or, worse, turn in the doorway and not come back for days. Then she had to make do with what she'd got and put up with the smell of old rubbish.

Sometimes Gösta's wife came down to get him, if she thought that he had been there for too long or she felt obliged to say something. Nothing pleased Ylva more. If Marianne came to get her husband, Ylva tripped around happily in the background, as if she was satisfied.

Marianne pretended not to see, but Ylva knew that it hit home.

Mike Zetterberg had stopped at a red light. He felt good, calm and strong. He always did when he came back from the hospital. He had been there five times now and was already much more stable than the first time he had gone to the clinic.

Gösta Lundin was a good doctor, considerate and kind. He called himself the Florida pensioner. He'd moved away from Stockholm in search of an easier life in his autumn years. Most Stockholmers chose Österlen, but Gösta and his wife couldn't see the point in living beside that brackish water where the algae flourished as soon as it was warm enough to swim in.

They were both happy with their choice and neither of them missed the capital. Except when the dialect became a bit too thick or the hostile comments about outsiders got too upsetting. In that sense there was a big difference between Helsingborg and Stockholm, Mike knew that only too well.

The pedestrians crossed the road in front of his car. Bodies moving, people on their way somewhere, a river. Mike was doing pretty well. Life had in some miraculous way taken over. He wouldn't say that he felt any less grief or that it had gone away, but it wasn't as all-consuming as before.

Sanna was happy, seemed to be almost unbelievably harmonious and unperturbed. Mike exchanged a few words with her teachers practically every day, but the many in-depth conversations from the period immediately after

Ylva's disappearance had now been replaced by something more akin to pleasantries.

'Everything okay?' Mike asked.

'Yes, we think so,' the staff said. 'She's a strong girl.'

His mother was an enormous support. Without her, it wouldn't have been possible. She collected Sanna from school and made supper several days a week. Sometimes she stayed over and cleaned the house the following day. Mike felt like a spoilt teenager, but he knew that the benefit was mutual. Kristina had lived up to her sudden importance.

They talked a lot about Mike's father, nearly more about him than about Ylva. Any talk of Ylva ended in guesswork and speculation, conjectures that didn't lead to anything positive, but that continued to ferment in his subconscious, only to surface a few days later as horrible dreams.

And on those nights, Mike couldn't get back to sleep. And then he sometimes phoned his mother and cried on the phone. They talked about grief and loss, about the awful feeling in your throat that made everything taste bad and that made it hard to breathe.

His mother and Gösta Lundin. Wise, understanding, sensible people who listened and let him talk, be miserable and weak. No bloody pills that calmed you down and took the edge off things.

Mike had to be clear-headed and present for his daughter.

It was his only obligation. And it gave him strength, this single priority. It had given him another perspective, he didn't care about anything else. His work was a means, not an end in itself. At meetings, he had started to ask the questions that no one else dared to ask, to raise obvious objections that normally were the remit of only the most powerful and influential.

Someone waved at him. One of the pedestrians had stopped in front of his car and was trying to catch his attention. A beautiful woman, who was smiling at him.

Was something wrong, Mike wondered, then he realised who it was and waved and smiled back.

Nour came over to the car and Mike opened the window on the passenger side. She bent down.

'Hi, how's things?'

He understood what she meant. They hadn't been in touch since all the drama in connection with Ylva's disappearance. Mike smiled at her.

'Good, thanks, everything's okay. Things feel much better, they really do.'

'I've thought about calling you a thousand times, but just never done it,' Nour said.

The car behind started to hoot. Mike glanced quickly in the rear-view mirror.

'I'm obviously in the way.'

'Where are you heading?' Nour asked.

'Work. And you?'

'Same direction. Can I get in?'

'Of course.'

Mike moved Sanna's booster. Nour opened the door and jumped in. Mike slipped into gear, but the car behind had already changed lanes and overtaken him, lights flashing furiously. Mike lifted a hand in apology, but the driver just shook his head.

'Urgent things,' Nour said, ironically. 'Really important things.'

38

The neon light on the ceiling flickered on and Ylva was woken by the sudden light. Her eyes were gungy and she felt feverish.

She didn't know how long the electricity had been off, but possibly a couple of days. The milk in the fridge had turned sour and the only thing she had to eat was dry, sliced rye bread and a cheap tin of tuna.

She didn't know why she was being punished. She had in fact anticipated some reward for her sexual services. She had done more than was expected of her and had really got into it. Gösta hadn't complained about anything.

Ylva looked at the screen. It was light outside and Mike's car wasn't in the driveway. She guessed it was a weekday.

Two hard knocks on the door. Ylva stood up on shaky legs and put her hands on her head. She was dizzy and felt her body swaying. To pass the time on the dark days, she had lain under the covers and hummed children's songs, over and over again up to ten thousand times, back and forth, and only stopped singing to go to the toilet.

Floor, walls, ceiling.

Now that the electricity was back on and she could follow the world outside via the TV screen, she was prepared to do almost anything to make sure it didn't go dark again.

She heard the key turning. The door opened and Marianne came in. She had a length of wound-up rope in her hand and Ylva automatically started to back away.

Marianne came towards her and Ylva sank down on to the bed, bowed her head and hunched her shoulders.

'Do you think I don't know what you're trying to do?'

Ylva looked up timidly without answering. The only words she was allowed to say without being told she could speak were thank you and sorry. And she had to say them wholeheartedly. If Marianne thought there was so much as the tiniest lack of sincerity, she would be punished.

'It's laughable,' Marianne said. 'You're a worthless whore and you think you can come between me and my husband. Do you have no grip on reality? Do you really think that he wants you?'

She paused, looked at Ylva with the same exasperation a teacher might show when dealing with a particularly stupid child.

'Do you honestly believe that anyone would want you? If we opened the door and let you go, what do you think would happen? Do you suppose Mike would take you back? When he finds out how shameless you've been in giving your body?'

Marianne sounded vaguely amused. Her derision was absolute because she knew she had total control. It was impossible for Ylva to contradict her. To even try answering back would be futile.

Marianne raised a hand. Ylva cowered instinctively.

'Why would I hit you?' she asked. 'It's not worth the effort.'

She threw the length of rope down on the bed and went back to the door. When she'd put the key in the lock, she turned round.

'Did I say that your daughter was here? I bought a May

Day flower from her. Gave her a bit extra. You might say that we're friends now.'

She opened the door and went out.

'South of Trädgårdsgatan,' Mike exclaimed, and turned, his eyes wide open.

'Scary?' Nour said, and tasted the coffee.

'Just a bit.'

'You better believe it. I grew up round here.'

'Impossible,' Mike said. 'One simply doesn't live south of Trädgårdsgatan, it's just not done.'

'Where did you grow up then?' Nour asked. 'Tågaborg?'

'Hittarp.'

'Really?'

Mike nodded and smiled.

'Back to the scene of the crime then, eh?' Nour said, and immediately regretted her choice of words.

'Suppose so,' Mike answered, without taking offence.

'Same house as well?'

'Not quite that bad.'

'Parallel street?'

Mike couldn't help laughing. It burst out through his nose.

'Almost,' he said.

Nour nodded silently to herself.

'I have a friend,' she said, 'who claims there are two ways of measuring a person's success. I can't remember what the first one is, but the second is the geographical distance between the place where you grew up and the place where you live now. The further the distance, the greater the success.'

'Then I'm a total failure,' Mike said. 'Though, having said that, I did actually live in Stockholm for a few years and I was born in the States.'

'A round of applause for you,' Nour said. 'And as soon as you had Sanna, it was home again?'

'Not for Ylva. She was from Stockholm.'

Was . . .

The unconscious choice of tense hung in the air.

Nour studied Mike, who swallowed nervously. Eventually she gave him a friendly smile.

'Do you think about her a lot?'

Mike pushed his cup into the middle of the table.

'I don't know what I think,' he said. 'I don't know if my thoughts have words. How do you think? In pictures or words?'

247

Nour didn't answer.

'She flickers by,' Mike said. 'Sometimes she has opinions. Stands beside me and says that I should turn down the heat so as not to burn the food, urges me to put my hands on my hips and roll my eyes when Sanna chooses the wrong clothes. What do you call that?'

'That she's watching over you?'

Mike took a deep breath and released it with a sigh.

'Whatever. Whatever the hell it is. Would you like to come for dinner?'

'Dinner?'

Nour jumped. The question was so sudden.

'If you've got a boyfriend, bring him with you,' Mike said.

'Yes.'

'Okay. Great. Friday?'

'I mean, I'd love to come. But on my own. I don't have a boyfriend . . .'

'Or should we say Saturday instead? If the weather holds, we could have a barbecue.'

Nour laughed. Mike had no idea why.

'What?'

'Barbecues.'

'Don't you eat meat?'

'Yes, yes, of course. It's just the whole idea. It's kind of, well, sweet.'

'Meat?'

'No, sweet. As in cute.'

'What's cute about a barbecue?' Mike wondered.

'Sweet, because it's touching,' Nour explained. 'Men who think they can do things. Like omnipotent children. All by themselves.'

39

Denial of the self

In order to cope with the humiliation and constant assaults, the victim learns to distance herself from her own body. It is not her who is being exploited, it is someone else. The body becomes a shell that has nothing to do with her. This extreme form of self-loathing can in time become so intense that the woman never finds her way back to her true self.

There was a knock at the door and Ylva positioned herself where she was visible and put her hands on her head.

The door opened and Gösta Lundin came in. He had a bag in his hand. Ylva tried to smile at him, but he glowered back at her.

'You're not wearing any make-up,' he said, and closed the door behind him.

'I'm sorry.'

Gösta pointed towards the bathroom and Ylva scurried in.

When she came out again, her lips were bright red and her eyes were smouldering. Gösta was standing beside the bed unbuttoning his shirt. He had already taken off his trousers and folded them on the edge of the bed.

'Down on your knees.'

Ylva kneeled in front of him and took hold of his underpants with both hands and teased them down as she beamed up at him. He tired of her play-acting, lifted his cock and thrust it into her mouth.

'Hands behind your back. Only your mouth. All the way in.'

Ylva clasped her hands behind her back and did as she was told. His cock swelled in her mouth and she wanted to pull back so she didn't choke, but Gösta grabbed hold of her head and pulled her towards him.

Ylva coughed, nearly threw up and instinctively turned her head away.

'I'm sorry,' she said.

Gösta pulled her up by the hair.

'Hands behind your back,' he reminded her when Ylva held on to the bed so it would be easier to get to her feet. 'Kneel on the bed.'

Ylva turned round and did as he said. Gösta pushed her forward so she fell with her face down on the mattress, this time without moving her hands.

'Keep your hands behind your back. All the time.'

When he was done, he shoved her to one side.

Ylva sat on the bed while he got dressed. The lipstick was gone, her eye shadow was smudged. It had been a long while since he'd been violent.

'My wife says you're getting sloppy.'

Ylva didn't understand.

'With the laundry,' Gösta continued. 'You only iron one side. That's not good enough, you have to iron the inside too.'

'I'm sorry.'

'I don't know what you do all day. And there's no feeling. I don't want to use violence, but won't hesitate to do it, if that's what's needed to get through to you.'

'I'm sorry.'

'You're starting to get ideas above your station. To think that you're important. Well, you mean absolutely nothing.'

He looked at her.

'Next time I expect you to take a bit of initiative.'

Gösta sighed and shook his head.

'And to think that Marianne and I had actually been discussing whether we should let you come up to clean the house.'

Nour handed over the present. Sanna took it with both hands and great delight.

'Can I open it?' she asked.

'Of course,' Nour said.

'But it's not my birthday.'

'It doesn't have to be your birthday.'

Sanna hurried out to the kitchen. Mike watched her go and then smiled at his guest. He gave her a cautious hug.

'Welcome.'

'Thank you,' she said, and produced a bottle of wine from her bag.

Mike took it and looked at the label.

'Not that expensive,' Nour said, 'but very good.'

'I'm sure it's good. Thank you. Can I take your coat?'

He hung up her coat and said she could keep her shoes on.

'But they're wet,' Nour said.

'No worries,' Mike insisted.

'Have you got a cleaner?'

'You make it sound like a bad thing.'

Mike put his hand to his heart and pretended to be upset. Nour stared at him. He smiled at her, but she didn't smile back.

'What?' Mike said, unnerved.

Nour shook her head.

'That was the last thing I heard Ylva say,' she said. 'We were going on about her coming out for one drink, and she said she wanted to go home. Someone shouted, "Say hi to the family," and she put her hand on her heart just like you did and said, "You make it sound like something bad."'

They stood in silence for a while, both surprised by how potent the memory was. Mike swallowed nervously.

'It's my mum,' he said, uncertain. 'Who cleans, I mean. I like to think she does it out of love.'

'She likes nothing more than to clean your house?' Nour teased.

'Who am I to deny her that pleasure?' Mike returned.

They went into the kitchen. Nour took a piece of kitchen roll and quickly wiped her shoes.

'I take it you're not intending to barbecue.'

'No, the weather certainly did change. So it's lasagne. Vegetarian. Hope that's okay?'

'Sounds good to me. Did your mum make it?'

'No, it was actually me . . . '

'Daddy! It's pens. And a drawing pad.'

Sanna held up her present.

'Yes. I seem to remember that you're very good at drawing,' Nour said. 'In fact, I still have your hippopotamus at work. Do you remember it?'

'It wasn't that good,' Sanna said.

'It's super good,' Nour told her. 'I look at it every day.'

Mike poured some wine and passed her a glass.

'Sanna, Coke?'

'Not just now.'

She wanted to try her new pens first.

'Well, cheers and welcome to our humble abode,' Mike said, and raised his glass.

They tasted the wine.

'Mm, lovely,' Nour said.

Mike looked at his daughter and mouthed *Thank you* to Nour. She shook her head. *It was nothing.*

'And thank you for coming,' Mike said. 'Sounds a bit

silly, but that coffee with you the other day made my week. What does that actually mean – "made my week"?'

'Enhanced?' Nour suggested.

'Yes. The coffee enhanced my week, it really did.'

Nour noticed that Mike's eyelashes were wet. He turned round and looked in the oven. Nour pulled out a chair and sat down beside Sanna.

'A cat?'

'Horse,' Sanna said.

'Yes, right, now I see it.'

Nour looked up. Mike had turned towards the work top and was blowing his nose.

'Hmm,' he said, and threw the tissue in the bin. 'I'm pretty pathetic really.'

He gave an embarrassed laugh.

'And you have every right to be,' Nour said.

40

'Three of the four are dead,' Jörgen Petersson said. 'That can't be a coincidence.'

Calle Collin didn't manage to hold back a sceptical laugh.

'You think there's a connection?' he chuckled. 'Morgan died of cancer, Anders was found murdered up by Fjällgatan, and Johan died in a motorbike accident in Africa. Now please explain the connection to me.'

'There's connection and there's connection,' Jörgen said. 'I see it more as proof that God exists.'

Calle held up his hand.

'You shouldn't say things like that, not even as a joke,' he said.

'But I mean it,' Jörgen told him in all seriousness. 'The world might not be better without them, but it certainly won't be as bad.'

Calle looked at him sternly.

'What did they do to you? How did they manage to leave such a mark that you can't even sympathise that they've lost maybe forty years of their lives?'

'Me?' Jörgen said. 'I kept out of the way as much as possible. But I still managed to get beaten up a couple of times. You could hardly say that they did any good. They terrorised everyone. The whole school bowed to their tyranny. I was terrified every time I had to go past them.'

'I don't remember it being like that.'

'How do you remember it, then?'

Calle shrugged.

'Last week I interviewed this guy who was paralysed from the waist down. He'd dived into shallow water and broken his neck. Eighteen years old. He was one of the most positive people I've ever met. I asked him whether he felt bitter about the fact that the accident happened to him. And do you know what he said? He said that there was no one else to blame, accidents like that usually happened to people who take risks, who expose themselves to unnecessary risks. He had only himself to blame, it wasn't even extreme bad luck. You should meet him. He might teach you a thing or two.'

'I'm sure,' Jörgen said.

Calle snorted in contempt.

'A wife and healthy children and pots of money. And you sit here whingeing about some idiotic losers who had their heyday in secondary school. And who are no longer with us. How many successful people do you know who were actually happy at school?'

'You're right,' Jörgen said. 'You're so right.'

'Of course I'm right.'

'But Ylva's still alive?'

'I don't know,' Calle said. 'Can't say that we're in daily contact. Haven't seen her since we were at school. I think she married someone from Skåne, or something like that.'

'Someone from Skåne?' Jörgen repeated.

'There you go,' Calle said. 'A fate worse than death.'

Jörgen stared blankly into space.

'Stop it,' Calle snapped. 'It doesn't suit you.'

Jörgen didn't understand.

'What?' he said.

'Sitting there ruminating.'

'I was just thinking—'

'Well, don't,' Calle interrupted. 'It won't do you or anyone else any good.'

Jörgen waved his hand around and crossed his legs.

'What you were saying,' Jörgen continued, 'about the boy who was paralysed, that it was self-inflicted . . .'

Calle wondered where he was going with this.

'Maybe it was the same with the guys in the Gang of Four,' Jörgen said.

'What do you mean?'

'Morgan got cancer, probably due to an unhealthy lifestyle. Anders was murdered in central Stockholm, and we can only guess the reason for that. And Johan was killed in a motorbike accident in Zimbabwe, and probably wasn't entirely sober at the time.'

Calle shook his head.

'You don't give up, do you?' he said.

'It's strange,' Mike said. 'I almost think more about Dad than I do about Ylva. All the old stuff bubbling to the surface.'

He was in Gösta Lundin's office on the fourth floor of Helsingborg hospital. Mike felt at ease in this setting and he had absolute confidence in his doctor.

'Do you mean, what could you have done differently?' Gösta asked him.

Mike cocked his head and pulled a face.

'It's not so much that, it's the feeling.'

'The feeling?'

'Just after it happened, a lot of attention was focused on my mother and me. Family, friends, Dad's funeral and all the details. Daily life was dramatic, heightened in some way. Maybe it sounds daft, but it was really exciting, a bit like the first day at school, or falling in love. Life was full of mean-ing, despite all the grief and helplessness. I presume that I . . . I don't know, felt important or something. God, I sound awful.'

'Not at all.'

'Because that's not what I mean.'

'I understand. Carry on.'

Mike gathered his thoughts, tried to formulate what he wanted to say.

'The other stuff came later,' he said.

'What other stuff?'

'The shame, the embarrassment, the looking away. People don't know how to deal with grief. There are so few who actually understand what you really need.'

'And what is that?' Gösta queried.

'Company,' Mike said, and looked at him. 'Or, at least, I think it is. Someone who asks you round for tea and is just friendly, normal, who calls and asks if you want to go to the cinema with them, who asks you to give them a hand with something. Whatever, just something to help the time go by.'

Mike smiled at his doctor.

'After all the rituals and stuff were out of the way, when everyday life had started to catch up and people expected you to be over it all, at that time, I would have appreciated even an inappropriate joke, anything, just not distance and silence.'

Mike laughed, looked at his hands and then raised his eyes again.

'I sound like some old talk-show presenter going on about his troubled childhood,' he said. 'And I assume that most people who sit in this chair do the same. You must think that we're a sorry bunch of moaning muppets.'

Gösta shook his head. He leaned forward and folded his hands on the desk.

'Your father,' he said in a friendly voice. 'Are you afraid that . . . well, that it's hereditary, shall we say? His depression, I mean.'

Mike shook his head and leaned back.

'Mum thinks it was the alcohol that killed Dad. It was a vicious circle. In the end she didn't know whether he was drinking because he was depressed or whether he was depressed because he was drinking. I'm pretty careful with alcohol, take after my mother in that regard. And as long as I've got Sanna, I would never even contemplate anything like that, never. Even though I must say I can understand Dad in a way, now. I mean, the pain was deep and the future was bleak. I understand why people commit suicide, I just don't want it to be those who are close to me.'

'What do you think happened to Ylva? Do you think she committed suicide?'

'No.'

'What do you think happened?'

'I think . . . '

He turned his face and looked at the wall.

'I think she was murdered. Possibly by accident. It might have been a sex game with the wrong person, a sexual assault, I don't know.'

'So you don't think she's alive?'

'No, I don't,' he said, after a while.

'You don't have any hopes left?'

Mike shook his head.

'I'd lose my mind then,' he said.

'Both the scenarios you mentioned involve sex,' Gösta pointed out.

'We've talked about that,' Mike said, curtly.

'Was she excessively flirtatious?'

'Yes.'

Mike had to strain himself to control his voice.

'And do you think that led her into the arms of the wrong person?'

'I have no idea any more. Ylva has gone, and she's never coming back. I actually don't want to think too much about what might have happened.'

'I'm sorry, I apologise,' Gösta said.

Mike pulled himself together and calmed down.

'Have you ever lost anyone close to you?' he asked, eventually, and locked eyes with the doctor.

'I had a daughter,' Gösta told him.

Mike's face shifted from angry to apologetic in a split second. Gösta held his gaze.

'It was twenty years ago. She was sixteen.'

'Cancer?'

Gösta didn't say anything for a long time.

'I'd rather not talk about it,' he said in the end. 'Not any more, and not with you. You're my patient, not the other way round.'

41

It wasn't good. Short contracts and the odd bit of freelancing. The only constant in Calle Collin's life was the bills. He expended more time and effort on picking up work than he did on doing it. He needed a steady job, regular pages to fill, someone to commission him to write a series of articles.

He logged on to the Internet and surfed in the hope of finding ideas. Death and misery, never anything else. That was basically all the news consisted of these days: unusual ways to die.

Which celebrities were hot? What was on TV?

What was it the old actor had said? That he beat others up so they wouldn't beat him. And of course he hadn't wanted the only interesting thing he'd revealed in the whole interview to be published in the magazine. Calle would have got more out of interviewing the actor's former classmates and writing about their recollections of him. Schooldays, childhood. You never got away from the past. Hence Jörgen Petersson's fixation with the Gang of Four.

The Gang of Four – three of the four were dead. Only Ylva was still alive. As far as Calle knew, anyway. Maybe he should interview her? Under the headline: *My Friends Die Young!*

She wouldn't have many friends left after an article like that.

On the other hand, it touched everyone. Who didn't know someone who'd died prematurely? Perhaps it wasn't such a bad idea. A series of articles about people who had died young and left family and friends bereft and mourning. What would it be called?

Out of the Blue. No, no, no. It needed to be something poignant. She Danced One Summer? Perhaps not. So a Day Passes, Never to Return? A Moment in Time? The Lord Giveth and the Lord Taketh? In Your Shadow? Garden of

Remembrance? Left Behind? The Days are Numbered? Seize the Day? It Happened Suddenly . . .?

Shit, come on.

Then the Game Was Over.

Calle mumbled the words to himself. Sounded good. Fatalistic, but still positive.

Then the Game Was Over.

Totally fucking perfect.

*

Future with no hope

A woman who succeeds in escaping from her captor has only a small chance of returning to her old life. It is of little consequence that she was forced into the situation; in most societies, it is still thought the woman has no one but herself to blame. She has brought dishonour on her family and often only a handful of her family and friends will be prepared to make the sacrifice needed to embrace someone who is a social outcast. As a result, the woman nearly always returns to her captor.

There was a world outside, and the only thing that separated Ylva from it was the cellar walls. She tried to remind herself of that, to recall the feeling she had had at first, before all her ambitions were thwarted. When she still imagined it was possible to escape. When she still tried to think logically.

Before she understood the price of her futile attempts, and the blows and threats had made her shrivel and accept. Her situation and who she was.

To clean the house.

The thought of being allowed up and being able to feel the sunlight had aroused something in her.

In her dreams, she jumped out of the window and ran across the grass to her own house and . . .

She never got any further. Her mind refused to dream on. Presumably it was trying to spare her the pain.

To clean the house.

They would never let her. It was just another way to torment her, a promise they waved in front of her eyes. They would snatch it away at the last minute. Just as they had done before.

Ylva looked around, thought about what was at risk, everything she had worked for.

The TV screen that gave her an eye on the world, food, water, electricity. Books to read.

The only thing they demanded of her was obedience. Otherwise, she was her own boss. The fact that Gösta took her body a couple of times a month didn't bother her any more. His pleasure showed that she was good. As long as Gösta wanted her, she was safe. As long as Gösta came back for more, she would be kept alive.

If that was what she wanted.

In her darkest moments, she thought about the rope. That was what Gösta and Marianne expected from her in the end. Eye for an eye, tooth for a tooth.

But Ylva wasn't there yet. And Gösta's half-promise about letting her up to clean the house had kindled a spark. She could almost visualise it. How, under supervision of course, she would go round with a vacuum cleaner and be blinded by the light that poured in through all the windows. Filled with colours and sounds from outside. Even in her dreams, Ylva felt overwhelmed.

She knew every nook and cranny of the cellar, every unevenness in the brickwork was etched in her mind. The cellar was her security.

Gösta seldom hit her. He only had to raise his hand. Ylva understood that he did it because it was necessary. To remind her who was in charge.

Marianne was worse, disdainful and patronising.

Sometimes Ylva fantasised that Marianne would die.

That it was just her and Gösta. She wished the plague on Marianne, that she would suffer, not a sudden accident. It would give her great pleasure if it was drawn out.

'You have to know your place,' Marianne said time and again.

'Don't forget what you are. An outlet for my husband's bodily fluids. Nothing more.'

The last time she was down in the cellar, she had grinned.

'I think you're dreaming about your old life. Yes. I do believe you are. That just shows how stupid you are. Have you looked at yourself in the mirror? If you were only half as ugly, it would be bad enough. I'm trying to come up with a word to describe what you are, but I can't. No, wait, I know. Spent. There you go. You're spent. Finished. You should think about the rope.'

Ylva tried to remind herself of something she'd heard Christians say. That you chose to believe.

She didn't believe. Not in the possibility of escape, nor that her old life was waiting for her outside.

To clean the house.

To be allowed to leave the cellar, if only occasionally. The thought made her giddy. It was almost impossible to take in.

Ylva's stomach was in upheaval.

She wished that Gösta hadn't said anything, not fed her that false hope.

Sanna watched them, as if she knew that Nour was a threat to her and Mike's world. But it was confusing for her, because she liked Nour and didn't know how to deal with the fact that her daddy also seemed to like her.

Sanna and Nour played badminton while Mike tended to the barbecue. Nothing to worry about. It was different later, when all three of them went to Hamnplan in the car to swim. Sanna insisted on sitting in the front as normal.

Mike said that the front seat was actually meant for adults, but Nour quickly and deftly managed to smooth feathers by jumping in the back.

Once they were in the water, Sanna showed all her tricks to Nour. She dived between her father's legs, jumped from the jetty and did the front crawl. But no matter how hard she tried, her father and Nour somehow seemed to end up beside each other all the time.

After swimming, they drove to Sofiero's and bought ice-cream, which they ate on the bench outside the kiosk. Sanna held out her cone so Nour could have a taste.

'Mm, that's good,' Nour said.

'What have you got?' Sanna asked.

'Rum and raisin. Do you want to try?'

Nour held out her cone and Sanna licked it.

'Ugh. That's horrible. Tastes like alcohol.'

'It is alcohol. Rum.'

'I'm not allowed that.'

'I think it's okay,' Mike said.

'Children shouldn't have alcohol,' Sanna said.

'No, that's right,' Nour replied.

'Why did you give me some then?'

'I thought you wanted a taste.'

'Not alcohol.'

'It's not real alcohol,' Nour explained. 'The raisins are soaked in rum for the flavour.'

'It tastes horrible.'

It was no more than that, but it was so pointed that Nour and Mike exchanged glances over her head.

'Will you drive me home?' Nour asked.

'Of course,' Mike said.

They dropped her off at Bomgränden. Nour stretched over from the back seat and put a hand on Mike's shoulder.

'Thank you for a lovely day.'

'Wait, I'll get out. We have to say goodbye properly.'

He got out of the car and gave Nour a hug.

'Thank you,' he whispered.

Nour patted him on the chest, bent down and spoke to Sanna.

'Have fun riding tomorrow. Hope to see you again soon.'

'Mm.'

In the car on the way home, Sanna asked her father if he was in love with Nour.

'Why do you ask that?'

Sanna shrugged.

'It seems like it.'

'Does it?'

Sanna didn't answer.

Mike drove home along Drottninggatan and Strandvägen. It was a meditative route that most people from Helsingborg preferred to the motorway by Berga. The sky was immense and open down by the water, whereas the motorway offered only traffic and movement.

Mike remembered the time when Tinkarpsbacken was still cobbled and how the sound changed when the car left the tarmac. Back then the trees in the avenue at the top of the hill were big and solid, the old king's sheep grazed in the meadow down by the water and there was a model of a sailing boat with several masts in the window of the red-and-white farmhouse closest to the road. Now the cobbles had been replaced by smooth tarmac, new trees, still pathetically small, had been planted on the avenue, and there was no longer a sailing boat in the farmhouse window.

'I miss Mummy,' Sanna said.

Mike glanced over at his daughter. She was staring straight ahead.

'I do too,' he said. 'I do too.'

42

'Karlsson speaking.'

'Hello. I'd like to remain anonymous.'

The voice belonged to a woman who was determined and yet unsure, given the situation.

'What's it concerning?' Karlsson asked.

'Ylva Zetterberg.'

'Who?'

'The woman from Hittarp who disappeared just over a year ago.'

'I'm with you,' Karlsson said. 'Why do you want to remain anonymous?'

'Because what I'm about to say is sensitive.'

'Well, come on then.'

'Ylva's husband is seeing another woman.'

Karlsson sat quietly and waited for her to go on, but she said nothing.

'And . . .?' he said in the end.

'He's spending a lot of time with one of Ylva's colleagues.'

'Right.'

'A *lot* of time, if you get what I mean.'

'They're an item?' Karlsson prompted.

'They're quite open about it, not ashamed. She's a foreigner.'

'Well, there you go.'

'My immediate thought was that they did it together.'

'Did what?'

'Got Ylva out of the way.'

'What makes you say that?'

'Like I said, just a thought. But perhaps it's not that interesting to you that the husband of a missing woman is having a relationship with one of her former colleagues?'

'All observations are of interest,' Karlsson said, and

rolled his eyes at Gerda, who had appeared in the doorway, eyebrows raised in question. 'I just don't quite understand why you think that they have anything to do with Ylva's disappearance.'

'Motive,' the woman said.

'Motive?' Karlsson repeated, and at the same time ceased to pay attention to the woman's ramblings.

'She stood in the way of their love.'

'Sounds fascinating,' Karlsson said. 'Is there a number I can get you on?'

'Yes, zero seven three – no, I want to remain anonymous, I said so.'

'Well, thank you for calling. I promise we'll follow that up.'

Karlsson put down the phone and looked at his colleague.

'The wife murderer in Hittarp,' he said. 'The man whose wife disappeared.'

'What did he want?' Gerda asked.

'No, no, it was some old cow, probably a neighbour. Apparently he's porking his wife's colleague.'

'Something we should check out?'

'How, exactly?'

'I don't know.'

'Precisely. Is there any fresh coffee?'

Virginia looked out of the kitchen window on to Tennisvägen. She held the teacup up to her mouth and blew. She had done the right thing. It would be wrong not to say anything. Wrong to stay silent. Mike shouldn't go unpunished.

It was three months since Nour had come over for dinner, two months since the first kiss, and so far they'd only managed to have sex a handful of times. Their initial attempt was more a case of clumsy groping while Sanna slept uneasily in the room next door. The other times had been up in Nour's flat on Bomgränden, at lunchtime.

This was the first night they had been alone together. Sanna had been packed off to her grandmother's.

The next day they had a leisurely breakfast before returning to the bedroom and exhausting each other of any energy they had left. Mike was feverish and his muscles ached after the unaccustomed exercise. He couldn't remember the last time he had felt so happy. It seemed years ago.

Mike phoned his mother and talked to Sanna. Officially,

he'd been at a work do. He could tell from the way his daughter chatted away that everything was fine. She and Granny had made dinner together and eaten in front of the telly, and Granny had read a whole book to her when she went to bed.

'... and now we're going to a ten-kronor shop in Denmark,' she concluded.

'So when do you want me to come and pick you up?'

'Not now. Later.'

'Okay. Can I speak to Granny?'

Mike agreed a time with his mother, finished the conversation and then turned to Nour.

'She doesn't want to come home,' he told her.

'Does that mean I can stay?' Nour asked.

Mike went over and kissed her.

'Shall we go out?'

'You mean for a walk?'

Mike nodded eagerly, like a child. Nour pulled her chin in.

'Is that fitting? Don't you need to sign the banns first?'

'Might as well take the bull by the horns.'

'Are you sure?'

Mike grabbed her hand and pulled her out into the hall.

'Come on.'

They walked side by side without holding hands. They obviously weren't out to exercise, but they didn't amble either; they strolled at a pace that might have suited a couple exercising an old dog.

When they reached the woods they kissed with such passion that neither of them could help laughing afterwards. They took each other by the hand, found a comfortable hold and carried on walking under the almost church-like green vault of beech trees towards Kulla Gunnarstorp. Once they had passed the ranger's red cottage and the fields opened out on both sides of the path, they let go of each other's hands.

'Does it feel inappropriate?' Nour asked.

'How do you mean?'

She shrugged.

'Maybe you feel that you ought to wear black for a bit longer.'

Mike shot her a swift look.

'She's not coming back,' he said.

They continued on along the path. Horses grazed in the fields and a southerly breeze whipped up white crests out on the sound.

'You're actually not really my type,' Nour said. 'I never

thought of you in this way before, when you were Ylva's husband. Now I just want to throw you over my shoulder, jump over the electric fence and have sex with you in that field. And I wouldn't give a toss if the whole town was standing round watching.'

Mike cupped her face with his hands and kissed her gently. He let his arms slip down her spine and held her tight. They stood in the middle of the path, their bodies swaying together. An elderly couple approached them from the north, but Mike didn't jump back. It wasn't until he saw who they were that he carefully disengaged himself.

'This is Nour,' Mike said. 'And this is Gösta and Marianne, they live opposite me on Sundsliden.'

They shook hands.

'Where's your daughter?' Marianne asked.

'Sanna?' Mike said. 'She's in Denmark with her grand-mother. They were going to some ten-kronor shop.'

Marianne was confused.

'Everything costs ten kronor,' Mike said. 'Or twenty. Inflation has caught up with the concept.'

Marianne gave an understanding nod. As if shopping was a suitable pastime for a girl of Sanna's age. Mike and

Nour said goodbye to the couple and carried on towards the castle.

'Gösta's the person I've been seeing,' Mike explained. 'The psychiatrist I told you about. Without him, I would never be where I am now.'

43

Mike was on his way to the hospital for another appointment with Gösta. It felt good. He knew already that he would feel even stronger when he left in a couple of hours' time. Gösta made him believe in life, made him believe that anything was possible.

It was of course a fleeting feeling that quickly faded and was swept away by the grey hard toil of everyday life, but with each visit, Mike inched his way up out of the darkest depths.

They didn't meet as often these days. Gösta reckoned there were others who needed his help more.

'Given what you've been through, you do seem remarkably well,' he had said before cancelling their regular appointments and starting to book Mike in for occasional sessions.

Now they only met every third or fourth week, and sometimes they spent the whole session just chatting, rather than delving into dark and troubling thoughts.

Mike was full of admiration for Gösta. Quite apart from his professional skills and the way he so wisely stepped back from life's worries, he was also a great example. Gösta had lost his daughter, survived his only child. Annika, as she had been called, would have been the same age as Ylva if she'd been alive. If either of them had been alive.

Mike had thought about it a lot. It must be unbearable to outlive your child. He couldn't imagine life without Sanna, refused to, and so pushed aside any such thoughts before they took root.

For twenty years, Gösta had struggled on, gone to work, listened to people's problems, tried to find solutions. He had never given in, become mean and bitter. Gösta and his wife had stuck together, supported each other and miraculously managed to carry on.

The Florida pensioners.

Mike wondered whether moving here had also been a way

to move on, to start afresh. It seemed strange that they'd waited twenty years before doing it, but perhaps they hadn't been able to leave until now. Houses and streets held great importance. Presumably they had felt they needed to stay until the memories faded and they were able to deal with them.

Annika had been sixteen when she died. Sixteen. She'd had her whole life in front of her.

Mike felt ashamed. He had thought he had a monopoly on suffering, had sat there wallowing, taking up space, almost bullish in his self-pity. Even though he knew that everyone had their dramas, that you only needed to scratch the surface with your fingernail.

And Gösta's loss was greater than Mike's.

'Well?' he said, as soon as Mike came into the room. 'Who is she, the woman you were holding hands with?'

Mike felt almost bashful.

'Nour,' he said. 'One of Ylva's old workmates. We ran into each other by accident, had a coffee. Then she came to dinner, and, well . . . '

'And, well . . . ' Gösta prompted, with arched eyebrows.

Mike smiled in response.

'Congratulations,' Gösta said. 'You deserve it. You see: life returns.'

'Yes, it does,' Mike said.

Gösta moved a piece of paper on his desk, put it on top of some other papers.

'So,' he said, with a friendly smile, folding his hands. 'What do you want to talk about today? Butterflies in your tummy?'

Mike laughed.

'Is it that obvious?'

'It's that obvious.'

'I never thought I'd feel like this again.'

'Life is strange.'

'I'm almost scared that it will pass,' Mike said. 'And it always does.'

'It can pass on into something else.'

'Yes, of course. And that's how it feels.'

'Well, there you go then. Nothing to talk about.'

'I don't think I felt like this even with Ylva.'

'Really?'

'Not this natural high, being in love.'

'What does Sanna think about it?'

Mike laughed and then looked at Gösta, serious again.

'You're amazing,' he said. 'You always put your finger on it. She was a bit wary at first. But that's so often the way with change. I think that's a very human trait, to be wary of change. Things are better now, though. The other night she even came in and lay between us in the bed. Almost like a family again.'

Gösta and Marianne were sitting at the kitchen table, drinking coffee and looking out of the window. They had both read the newspaper that lay on the table between them.

'I don't know,' he said. 'It seems . . . I don't know.'

He looked at his wife.

'You think that we should carry on living like this?' she said.

Now it was Gösta's turn not to say anything. Not for tactical reasons, but because he couldn't. He couldn't live up to his wife's expectations.

'You like it,' she said, full of reproach.

'I don't.'

'Yes, you like it. And what's worse, she likes it. The little cunt thinks you're a couple, you and her. I don't think she's ever going to commit suicide. You should rape her, not satisfy your own needs.'

Gösta shook his head.

'Stop it,' he said.

'Stop it?'

She glared at him. 'She's going the same way as Annika. Have you forgotten that? She'll take her own life. And if she doesn't do it of her own accord, then we'll have to help her fit the noose.'

Gösta sat in silence. Marianne looked up at the ceiling and breathed deeply until she was calm again.

'How long do you intend to keep this up?' she asked, eventually. 'It won't work, you must realise that. It's a miracle that it's worked until now. You can't blame me for thinking that you're drawing it out for your own sake.'

'Stop!'

Gösta slapped his hand on the table, but it was a feeble gesture. Marianne chose not to remark on it, and instead waited for him to speak.

'I want the same as you,' he said. 'I just don't see how. Practically, I mean.'

Marianne shrugged.

'A tiled bathroom,' she said.

Gösta took a deep breath and stared out of the window. Marianne studied him. He looked out of sorts.

'Good God,' she said. 'This is hardly the time to be lily-livered.'

She stood up, and took the coffee cups over to the sink.

44

Ylva was so close to the screen that the picture was fuzzy. She took half a step back and refocused.

Nour was at home with Mike. She was playing badminton with Sanna, without a net. Their enthusiasm was greater than their skill.

Nour was wearing shorts and a bikini top, not the clothes she'd had on when she arrived. Sanna was relaxed and happy, Nour playful and lively. At home, and yet not.

The relationship with Mike was blossoming. Nour was starting to take her place.

There was a knock at the door.

Ylva hurried over to where she had to stand, put her hands on her head, pouted and pulled back her elbows to push out her bust, like he said she should.

She was made up and ready, in her underwear and high heels. It was an arranged visit and Gösta Lundin had told her what he wanted.

He closed the door behind him, placed a bag of food on the worktop, then came over to her. He gestured for her to get down on her knees and she instantly obeyed.

She moaned in anticipation as if she wanted him to fill her. He undid his belt and unzipped the fly.

She took his penis and put it in her mouth, then splayed her painted nails like a porn star. He was quick to harden. She looked up and saw his disdainful expression. He grabbed her hair and pulled her head back and forth.

'Play with your pussy, I want you wet.'

She put her hand down her knickers, touched herself, felt the lubricant she had rubbed on and moaned as she had learned.

Afterwards, he noticed she was interested in what was going on on the screen. He wondered whether she still imagined, hoped, planned.

'Your husband has been coming to see me,' he said.

Ylva stared at him.

'For several months now. Some crazy woman at a party accused him of being responsible for your disappearance. Claimed that everyone else thought the same, that he was involved.'

Gösta laughed.

'Funny. He could cope with you disappearing, but not with innocent accusations and gossip.'

The new information made Ylva's head spin. It was the same horrid feeling she'd had when Marianne told her that she'd bought May flowers from Sanna. Mike was Gösta's patient, he discussed his innermost feelings with him, opened himself to the man who was holding her prisoner and who had raped her systematically and ritually for over a year. Ylva was not the only victim. Gösta and Marianne's abuse had spilled over on to her family.

She felt his hand on her stomach. Stroking her, moving up to her breasts. Ylva hated him touching her afterwards more than anything. When it should be over, but carried on all the same.

This time it was worse than ever.

And yet she still did exactly what was expected of her, lowered her eyelids and moaned with pleasure.

He moved his hand down between her legs, felt the wetness. Lubricant and sperm.

'We talk a lot, your husband and I. He's full of admiration for me. He asked if I'd lost anyone, so I told him about Annika. For obvious reasons, I didn't go into details. Your husband said that my loss was greater than his, that he couldn't imagine losing his daughter.'

Gösta lay quietly for a while.

'And I have to agree with him,' he said, and rapped Ylva on the hip. 'Turn round, I want to take you from behind.'

Family Journal was interested. They were happy with Calle Collin's last job, and had already talked about inviting him down to Helsingborg for a meeting with the editors to discuss more regular work. When he presented his idea for *Then the Game Was Over*, the matter was clinched. Calle's flight to Ängelholm was paid for and he took a taxi to the big, silvery grey publishing house on the southside of Helsingborg.

The managing editor showed him round and gave him lunch in the staff canteen. Because the subject matter for his proposed series would be highly sensitive, she wanted more details.

Calle suggested that, following a couple of introductory articles, they should, as far as possible, let the readers approach them, and not chase anything or go looking for names in old death notices. As the person who had died was to be portrayed by a family member or friend, the perspective would vary. It might be about the grief of losing a spouse, or a child, a parent, a sibling, a friend. They should try to keep the tone as objective as possible, as the contrast with the heartbreaking story would maximise the impact. Each article would include a brief biography of the deceased, a detailed account of events leading up to their death, the interviewee's favourite memory of their lost loved one, and a few interesting details from the life that had ended. The sort of thing that was never given space in or was deemed unsuitable for more traditional reports.

'When the readers put down the magazine, I want them to understand that this great tragedy could strike any one of our family or friends at any moment,' Calle explained. 'I want them to feel the need to give their nearest and dearest a good long hug.'

The managing editor studied his face, as if she was trying to gauge whether he was being ironic or not. When she was convinced of his sincerity, she gave a decisive nod.

'How did you get the idea?' she asked.

Calle told her about the Gang of Four, the tyrants from his past, who had fallen, one by one, until now there was only one left.

'In fact, she and her husband live here in Helsingborg. I thought I could look her up and see what she knows.'

Calle had got her married name from the tax register. Then he'd found the address and her husband's name on the Internet.

'For the series?' the managing editor asked, horrified.

Calle realised that bullies and nasty sudden deaths were not high on the list of dream articles. She looked at him again with renewed suspicion.

'No, no,' Calle assured her. 'It just struck me as odd. Three out of four. Did they lead harder lives? Did they court death? It's not really directly related to my idea, I just thought it would be interesting to meet her again. After all these years. It's a long time since we last met.'

He put on a bright smile, but the managing editor was still sceptical. Who wanted to meet bullies from their past?

'She lives just outside town,' Calle carried on, to fill the awkward silence. 'Hittarp, or thereabouts.'

'Oh, I live there,' the managing editor said. 'What's her name?'

'Ylva,' Calle replied. 'She's married to someone called Michael Zetterberg.'

The managing editor stared at him, aghast, her eyes wide open.

Something was wrong, Calle realised that much. Something was very wrong.

45

Calle was sitting on a yellow bus on his way into the centre of Helsingborg. He was finding it hard to swallow, his face was flushed and he thought about his wealthy friend, Jörgen Petersson. Who was he, really? He could obviously be tough and cold when it came to business. Rich people were their money, their bank balance was their identity. That's how they defined themselves. But it was quite a leap from there to believing that you could play with life and death . . .

Calle went to the front to speak to the bus driver.

'Excuse me, a quick question. How do I get to Hittarp?'

'Well, you take the 219,' the driver said with a thick Skåne dialect.

'And where does that go from?'

'Well, you're on it.'

'So this bus goes to Hittarp?'

'Well, either that or it's not the 219.'

Calle didn't understand. Was the bus driver taking the piss?

'So you go to Hittarp?' Calle insisted.

'Well . . .'

'I don't understand,' Calle said. 'Is this some kind of a joke?'

'Well, I'm joking with you a wee bit. But you can take a joke up there in Stockholm, can't you?'

'Can you just let me know when we get to Hittarp, please?'

Calle sat down again. He could never live outside the capital.

'We should talk to the bastard,' Gerda said.

'Why?' Karlsson wanted to know.

Gerda shrugged.

'He might be ready to tell us what actually happened.'

'Big risk,' Karlsson said. 'He's fallen in love and has a daughter to look after. Why are there never any pastries? Only those God-awful biscuits that are so dry that you have to drink something just to be able to swallow them.'

'Maybe he didn't do it,' Gerda suggested.

'Who? What?'

'That upper class twat. He could be innocent.'

Karlsson laughed.

'Yeah, right. A regular Snow White. What was it she said?'

'Who?'

'That actress?'

'I don't know what you're talking about.'

'You know,' Karlsson continued. 'The blonde one who sounded like a transvestite. Old black-and-white films.'

'Rita Hayworth?'

'She didn't sound like a tranny. Before that. Hands on her hips, crude as hell.'

'Marilyn Monroe?'

'No, not Marilyn Monroe. I said earlier. The first talkies, around then.'

'No idea.'

'Mae West.'

'What about her?'

'She said it.'

'Said what?'

'"I used to be Snow White, but I drifted." Bloody brilliant.'

'I don't get it,' Gerda ventured.

'I used to be Snow White, but ... okay, she's not any more.'

'I used to ...?'

'... be Snow White, but I drifted.'

'What does she mean, "drifted"?'

'I know what it means, I just don't know how else to put it.'

Gerda nodded. 'Okay.'

Calle got off the bus. The first thing he saw was two girls, early teens, riding slowly past on their ponies. Then a single car crept up the hill. He could see Öresund and the Danish coastline through the gaps between the houses.

Calle read the road names: Sperlingsvägen, Sundsliden. He took out the map he had printed off from the Internet and tried to work out where he was. An elderly woman was raking the gravel in her driveway. Calle nodded to her.

'Do you need any help?' she asked, in a Stockholm dialect.

'No, thank you. I think I know where I'm going.'

Calle raised a hand in thanks. Stockholmers were good people, he thought to himself. The woman smiled at him again, and it seemed to Calle that she was familiar in some way. But friendly faces often are.

'Where are you going?' she asked.

'Gröntevägen,' Calle told her.

'It's just over there, on the other side of the grass. Are you looking for someone in particular?'

'Michael Zetterberg,' Calle said.

'He lives in the big white house with a black roof.'

The woman pointed in the general direction.

'Thank you,' Calle said, and started to walk.

He was about to turn round and ask if they'd maybe met before, but, given what the managing editor of *Family Journal* had just told him, he wasn't in the mood for small talk.

Ylva had disappeared nearly a year and a half ago. Three of the four were dead, and the fourth was missing. What did it all mean? Was there a connection? Or was it just coincidence?

Calle walked along the road, resisting the temptation to

cut across the grass. It was bound to be wet, and he had put his best shoes on in honour of the meeting, even though they were actually a bit thin for the cold autumn weather.

The Zetterbergs' house was big, and the garden looked well tended. When Calle got closer he noticed a trampoline that had obviously been left out over winter, a forgotten football and a kick-sledge that had been abandoned by the terrace door.

Good, Calle thought to himself. You had to watch out for people who were too fussy. He had written enough articles for interior design magazines to know that the coolest houses and apartments smelled of chlorine and divorce.

The driveway was empty.

Calle went up to the door and rang the bell. No one at home. In a way, he felt relieved. He had no idea what he would say to Ylva's husband.

Calle looked at his watch, quarter past five. He had booked a ticket for the last flight, precisely so he could interview Ylva. Contrary to what he'd told the managing editor at *Family Journal*, he had of course thought of using the material. A young and beautiful woman who'd lost three of her closest friends from school – that was just the kind of thing readers wanted.

But now, she wasn't available. So Calle wanted to talk to her husband instead.

About what?

He felt uneasy. Was he really just a parasite, feeding on other people's misfortune? He decided to go for a walk in the neighbourhood to clear his mind.

There were houses everywhere. Lots of old villas, and some new builds with huge glass fronts.

He headed towards the water, noted a vast, forbidding house on the hill to the left, and the smell of seaweed. When he got to the shore, he decided that fibre-cement roofing didn't look so bad after all, before turning right in the direction of two jetties. He felt compelled to go out on to one.

He stood at the end of the jetty. To his right lay the Kattegatt, straight ahead the Danish coastline, and to his left the ferry lane between Helsingborg and Helsingör. And beyond that, he could see the island of Ven.

No more than an hour ago, he'd sworn that he would never move out of central Stockholm, but now he found himself wondering whether he should revise that decision. The sky was endless and full of promise. Calle understood why people who had grown up here might find it hard to leave the place. A seagull sailed deftly past on the wind and seemed to mock him with laughter. Calle turned and retraced his steps.

He carried on north along the water and then up a long slope. He eventually managed to find his way back to Gröntevägen where a car was now parked in the driveway.

Calle hesitated. What was he going to ask?

A man who was grieving for his missing wife. She went out to buy a newspaper and never came back . . .

Dot, dot, dot.

It was a story, no doubt about it.

But a delicate situation: the woman had disappeared, which automatically made the husband a suspect. The man was always the villain.

How was he going to approach this?

The Gang of Four, obviously. Only he wouldn't call them that in front of the husband.

Calle swept his thoughts to one side. He didn't need a plan, he was a reporter, a journalist for a weekly, you couldn't get more hard-boiled. Just a shame that the rest of the world didn't understand that.

He rang the bell and heard the light footsteps of a child hurrying. A girl opened the door and looked up at him, face full of expectation.

'Hi, is your dad home?'

'Yes.'

She turned and ran towards the kitchen.

'Daddy!'

Mike had an apron on and was drying his hands on a dishcloth. He looked questioningly at Calle, who held out his hand and flashed him what in his mind was an irresistible smile.

'Calle Collin. Hello.'

'Hi,' Mike said, cautiously.

He wasn't sure who he had in front of him. A Jehovah's Witness?

His daughter looked on with interest.

'I went to Brevik School on Lidingö,' Calle said. 'I was there at the same time as Ylva. I heard that she was missing and I wondered if I could come for a chat.'

Mike cleared his mind. He hesitated for a moment or two, then shook it off.

'Yes, of course.'

46

Ylva saw that Mike and Sanna had come home for the evening and switched to a TV channel. Gösta had connected her only a few months ago. The TV was her greatest luxury and she often left it on. For some company and noise, if nothing else.

At this time in the afternoon, they showed old sitcoms. Ylva loved the studio laughter, it made her feel all warm.

She had ironed the day's laundry and had even managed to polish a couple of candlesticks – in other words, she'd accomplished quite a bit.

It was well into autumn now, and Ylva had long since

laid her plans to escape on hold. She was undeniably an idiot, just as Gösta said. He was happy enough with her sexual performance, though; he even said she was a natural talent, born to it.

'But you get a lot of practice, too.'

She thanked him, mustered the courage to ask if they might let her clean the house, after all. She promised she'd do a good job.

He said he'd think about it. Ylva felt certain that sooner or later she'd be given the chance. He had been generous recently, spoiling her with food and books.

There wasn't any reason, really, to risk it all by trying to escape.

'Wait, wait, wait.' Mike held his hands up in front of him.

Calle Collin stopped talking. He'd told Mike the background, that his original intention had been to interview Ylva about the fact that three of her classmates had died so young, but then the managing editor for *Family Journal*, who lived locally, had told him that Ylva had been missing for more than a year.

'So you're a journalist,' Mike said, and looked very disapproving.

'For the weeklies,' Calle said. 'I'm not a news reporter.'

'And you want to write about dead people?'

'Well, yes . . . no. But . . . '

'But what?' Mike said. His face was bright red and his daughter looked at him with a worried expression.

'I just think it all seems a bit odd,' Calle said.

'What?' Mike barked.

'That three out of four are dead and the fourth is missing.'

'What are you talking about? Three out of four? Three out of four what?'

'The Gang of Four,' Calle said, and looked down at the table, embarrassed.

'The Gang of Four?' Mike repeated, shaking his head.

Calle met his eyes. It was now or never.

'Ylva used to hang out with these three guys: Johan Lind, Morgan Norberg and Anders Egerbladh. The four of them terrorised the school. Morgan died of cancer. Anders was murdered in Stockholm. Johan died in a motorbike accident in Africa. I wondered if there might be a connection. With your wife's disappearance.'

The girl turned to her father, looked at him in suspense.

The veins on Mike's forehead were throbbing, his chest

was heaving, his lips were tight. When he spoke, it was in a very low voice, almost a whisper.

'I have never heard anything about the individuals you've just mentioned, so I assume that they can't have made much of an impression on my wife. And if you don't leave people alone to grieve in peace, I'll have something to say to your boss at *Family Journal*. In fact, I think I will anyway. And now I want you to stand up and get out of my house and never show your face here again.'

'But, but, I just—'

'Now.'

Calle got up and left.

47

Calle Collin rested his forehead on the window of the airplane, felt the cold plastic against his skin. The plane accelerated down the runway and he was pushed back into his seat. He wasn't a frequent flyer and by this point in the flight his mind would usually be racing through scenarios where the plane would crash, killing everyone on board. Most of these had the plane breaking in two in mid-air, and the passengers being sucked out into the dark, cold air, where they floated helplessly just long enough to reflect on their sins, before plummeting to the ground.

But this time, Calle's head was full of other scenes. He

imagined Michael Zetterberg contacting the managing editor of *Family Journal*. Maybe he'd call her, or just bump into her on a Sunday walk. And then he would tell her what had happened. That some crazy reporter from Stockholm had looked him up, wanting to talk about Ylva's disappearance. He'd implied that Ylva hadn't been the nicest of girls and then he'd mentioned a bunch of dead classmates and generally been rather unpleasant.

What's more, this individual said that he was working for *Family Journal*. Was that true?

Calle could just imagine the managing editor listening carefully, her anger rising, and then saying that she did in fact know who Ylva's husband was talking about, and that it was totally out of order and she promised, promised, to contact the reporter immediately and put a stop to all this nonsense.

The next scene that filled Calle's mind was the telephone conversation that would ensue: the bollocking he'd get, his contract terminated. Then the gossip.

That Calle Collin, what happened to him? He used to be a really good journalist and a decent guy. Evidently he's lost it completely now.

His third thought, and by this time the plane had landed and was taxiing towards the gate at Arlanda, was Jörgen. That terrible man with his pockets so full of money that he had nothing better to do than to cultivate the self-invented myth that he was an interesting eccentric.

It was his fault. Everything. Even if he wasn't exactly behind it all.

Instead of waiting for the bus, Calle hopped into a taxi.

'Lidingö, please.'

He turned on his mobile and called Jörgen.

'I'm on my way over,' Calle said. 'We need to talk.'

'There was someone here today,' Marianne said.

'Here?' Gösta asked.

'Here, on the street. He asked where Gröntevägen was. He was going to see Mike. Called him Michael.'

'Right.'

Gösta sounded vaguely interested, but carried on looking through the paper.

'Gay,' Marianne said. 'He was their age, spoke with a Stockholm dialect.'

'A poof from Stockholm, stop the press.'

Marianne sighed, tired of her husband.

'There was something about him,' she said. 'It was almost like he recognised me.'

'Did he introduce himself?'

'Of course not.'

'Did he say anything?'

'No.'

'Well then.'

Marianne got to her feet, annoyed, and started to load the dishwasher. Gösta carried on reading the newspaper without paying her much attention. She slammed the door shut in irritation. Gösta looked up.

'We can't carry on like this for ever,' she said. 'We're almost done, there's only Ylva left. We have to finish it and we have to do it now.'

48

Calle Collin paid the taxi driver, went to the gate and rang the bell. He looked up at the camera. The intercom crackled.

'Come in,' Jörgen said, and the lock clicked.

Calle pushed open the gate and made his way to the house. Jörgen had opened the front door before he even got there.

'To what do I owe the honour?'

Calle looked at his old school friend intently.

'Is the family home?'

'Of course,' Jörgen said.

'Then I suggest we take a walk.'

Jörgen didn't know why, but he nodded.

'I'll just get a jacket,' he said.

As soon as they were through the gate, Calle grabbed hold of Jörgen's collar and pushed him up against the well-trimmed hedge.

'What the hell have you done? Have you killed them all?'

Jörgen looked shocked. He blinked rapidly and his lower lip trembled.

'For Christ's sake, let me go. What are you talking about?'

'You've killed them,' Calle yelled. 'All of them.'

'Who? What are you talking about?'

Jörgen was on the verge of tears. Calle held on to him.

'Do you think I don't realise? You've got so much money that you think you have the power to decide who lives and who dies. Who are you going to bump off next? Am I safe? Or maybe you want to kill me too?'

'Shut up, Calle. I haven't done anything. What are you going on about?'

Calle was shaking, his body so tense that he felt he would explode. Jörgen was gasping for air and crying openly, the snot running from his nose. Calle pushed him further back into the hedge.

'I'll go to the police, you can be bloody certain of that,' he said. 'I'm going to tell the police.'

'I h-haven't done anything,' Jörgen stammered.

Calle pushed him away and started to walk. He'd gone no more than five metres when he stopped and turned back. He stretched out a hand and helped his friend to his feet and then hugged him, the tears streaming. They walked to the house arm in arm.

'Are you playing *Brokeback Mountain?*' asked Jörgen's wife.

Calle laughed. 'No, I've still got some standards.'

Jörgen's wife pulled in her chin. 'Unlike me, you mean?'

Jörgen kissed her carefully on the cheek.

'Calle's just jealous,' he said.

They went upstairs and sat in the kitchen. Calle told Jörgen about his day in northwest Skåne, and about Ylva having disappeared without a trace nearly eighteen months ago.

'But she can't just have vanished?' Jörgen said.

'Her husband must have killed her,' his wife chipped in.

Calle shook his head.

'If he was guilty, he wouldn't have thrown me out. He

would have welcomed anything that pointed the finger at someone else.'

Jörgen's wife got up with a sigh.

'You two sound like real numpties. There's no connection between any of the dead people other than that they went to school together.'

'The Gang of Four,' Jörgen said.

His wife rapped him on the head.

'Stop it,' she said. 'You've got Calle going. Now listen here, both of you. You can't carry on like this. You need to get a hobby, have an affair or something.'

'Yes, I'll have to think of something to do,' Calle said. 'Because I won't be getting any more work, that's for sure.'

There was a knock and Ylva stood where she was visible with her hands on her head. The door opened. It was Marianne. Ylva knew it. Her window on the world showed that it was daytime, not much going on. Gösta was at work.

Marianne closed the door and came into the room. She had a plate with her.

'There was some left over,' she said.

Ylva took a step towards her.

317

'Stay where you are,' Marianne said, and held up her hand.

Ylva stood still.

'Sit.'

Ylva obeyed.

Without taking her eyes off her face, Marianne scraped the leftovers from the plate on to the floor.

'Do you think this is dignified?' she asked.

Ylva didn't answer.

'You're a dog. The question is, what kind of dog? The small, yapping kind, or the big, lumbering kind? Doesn't really matter though, they all smell disgusting. I have to say, you're costing us a lot of money. Electricity, food and I don't know what. You're not exactly worth the money. No, I reckon we're getting to the end of the road. Don't you agree?'

Ylva looked up at her, puzzled.

'That's a good girl, clever dog, you understand exactly what your mistress is saying. You should do what Annika did. Follow her example. It's for the best. I mean, this isn't life, is it? Not for you, not for anyone. And we both know that you don't deserve any better, I think we can agree on that.'

Marianne gave a resigned sigh.

'Think about it,' she said.

She went back to the door, opened it, and turned round.

'If the rope's not enough, I can get some pills for you.'

She nodded at the food on the floor.

'Go on, eat your food.'

49

Mike rang and said it was an emergency, asked if he could come. And Gösta of course made the time.

'Tell me,' he said, and Mike told him about the mysterious visit.

Gösta listened and smiled in amusement, and Mike grew more and more uncertain.

'What is it?' he said, feeling like a child who was being indulged.

'I thought it was something serious,' Gösta said.

'But, Jesus, it is serious.'

'No,' Gösta countered, 'it's not serious. How are things with Nour?'

'Good, good. What do you mean, it's not serious?'

'I thought your love life was falling to bits,' Gösta said. 'But this is no more than a wasp at a picnic. Annoying, yes, and difficult to brush off, but you're still having a picnic.'

Mike allowed himself to be calmed, and, after a while, he laughed too.

'But you must admit, it is strange.'

'What? That some old school friends have died of cancer or in an accident? You said yourself that Ylva had never mentioned them. Can hardly have been close friends. So, what have we got? Three people who have died, who all went to the same relatively big school. I don't see what the issue is.'

'They were in the same class,' Mike said. 'And the guy too. The one who came to see me.'

Gösta didn't say anything.

'Should I go to the police?' Mike asked.

'What for?'

'To report him. Next time he might touch up Sanna.'

Gösta lifted his eyes to the ceiling, clenched his lips and rolled his head backwards and forwards while he thought.

'I don't know,' he said. 'Do you think there's any real danger?'

'Nothing direct,' Mike said. 'Hard to say. But I would never forgive myself if something happened to her.'

Gösta leaned across the desk.

'What did you say he was called?'

'Calle Collin.'

'Have you googled him?'

'He's written articles for a number of papers and publications, nothing weird.'

'You said that he was working for *Family Journal*. Maybe you could talk to someone there first?'

'What was he called? Calle . . .?'

Marianne looked impatiently through her daughter's old yearbook. She ran her finger down the list of names.

'Calle, Calle, Calle. Jonsson?'

'No, Collin,' Gösta corrected.

'Here,' she said, and read out: 'Third from left, second row. There.'

She studied the photograph, looked doubtful, shrugged.

'I would never have recognised him,' she said.

The doorbell rang. Gösta leaned forward, looked out through the window and saw that it was Mike.

'Jesus, it's him.'

'Well, go and open the door then,' Marianne hissed.

Closing the door to the cellar, to be on the safe side, Gösta made his way to the front door. He opened it, feigning surprise. Mike was standing there with a bottle in his hand.

'A symbol of my gratitude,' he said.

'Oh, you shouldn't have. There was really no need.'

'Yes, you've meant an enormous amount to me. I don't know how I would have managed without your help.'

Gösta took the bottle, looked at the label and raised his eyebrows in appreciation.

'Goodness. Well, thank you very, very much. This is more than enough, but thank you. I would ask you in, but now's not really a good time.'

'No, no, don't worry, I have to go home and rustle up some food for Sanna,' Mike said. 'I just wanted to give you that, no more.'

'Thank you,' Gösta said again.

'No, it's me who should thank you.'

Mike gave a wave and left. Gösta closed the door and went back to his wife in the kitchen.

'He recognised me,' she said, and tapped her finger on the photograph in the school yearbook. 'I don't think he managed to place me, but when he does, he'll no doubt put two and two together.'

'Relax. Why do you want to believe it's worse than it is? First of all, why should he recognise you? How many of your school friends' parents would you recognise? And you didn't recognise him.'

'No, but that's because he was a child then and now he's an adult. I'm sure we've changed a lot too, but not in the same way.'

Gösta sighed.

'And even if he did recognise you, why would he make the connection with Ylva? There's no reason. Besides, Mike threw him out. It's not very likely that Calle Collin will contact him again.'

'Perhaps not, but there's a risk.'

Marianne took a deep breath.

'Gösta, it's time. She has to go. If she doesn't do it herself, you'll have to help her.'

Ylva saw it all on screen.

Mike strode over towards the house where she was, a bottle of wine in his hand. Soon after, he left again, empty-handed.

The camera didn't cover the area outside the front door, but it didn't require much imagination to guess what had happened. Mike had come to give them a bottle of wine. Which confirmed what Gösta had said: that he and Mike were close, that Gösta had Mike's ear.

The wine was obviously a thank you for his help. For listening to Mike, even though it happened to be his job. That was the way it worked in the suburbs, a bottle of wine in return for a friendly gesture. Between neighbours.

Ylva wondered what it would mean for her. What dangers it might entail. Gösta and Marianne could not, under any circumstances, entertain in their house. Anyone who crossed the threshold was a risk to them. They had to keep their distance from any neighbours who tried to get closer; they could greet them cheerily but no more than that.

Gösta's interest in her had waned, Ylva was very aware of that. She knew that the day he no longer wanted her, she was lost.

Ylva tried to moan with more feeling and to reinvent herself in every thinkable way, but still Gösta seemed to be bored. It was really only when he took her with force that he managed to muster the same interest that he'd shown in her for the first six months.

50

It was important that they didn't get carried away. They had to plan it, weigh up every alternative carefully. It wouldn't be any problem to kill her. But Gösta still believed that they could persuade her to take that step herself. They simply had to open her eyes, force her to recognise her situation and fully understand what she had become. Then she would see that there was only one thing left for her to do.

No, the problem was how to dispose of the body and hide the evidence.

If he had a boat, he could dump her in the sea. But then again, how would he get to the boat with a black rubbish bag over his shoulder without anyone noticing? There were houses all the way down. You'd be hard pushed to find a stretch of coastline that was more guarded. And no matter which rough track he took through the woods, there was always the risk that some outdoor type would be there looking for mushrooms, and would see the car and remember the registration number.

Burying the body would be heavy work and the chances of it being discovered were considerable.

Why try to hide the body? Surely the best thing would be if it was found as quickly as possible. Then Mike could bury her in the ground and finish grieving. Be free of other people's suspicion. Even if that meant a lot of help and therapy when Mike discovered that Ylva had been alive the whole time she'd been missing.

The best thing would be for them to dump the body in a ditch alongside some deserted road. He could choose the time rather than the place. At night, when no other headlights were in sight. Then he would quickly toss the body and drive on. It would have to be done in conjunction with some bona fide trip, something that would provide him with an alibi in the unlikely event that he ever came under suspicion.

The body would be wrapped in black bin liners so that no traces were left in the car. They would have to scrub under her nails and he wouldn't be able to come inside her in the final days. The latter would mean a bit of a sacrifice on his part.

While Gösta was out dumping the body, Marianne would stay at home and clear the cellar. Every surface would need to be cleaned and the furniture replaced with a suitable drum kit and electric guitar.

They would have to draw up a plan and decide on the date.

Gösta wondered how it would feel to be without Ylva. A relief, obviously, when it was over. But also quite sad.

Avenging Annika had been their driving force for nearly three years. The fight for justice and retribution had overshadowed almost everything. The goal had been clear and life had, in a way, been simple.

Soon it would be over, leaving a vacuum that opened up like an abyss.

The possibility of going down to fuck Ylva whenever he pleased had given him a feeling of richness. An extra dimension.

Soon that would also be history.

Was wine too little? Surely not? The bottle had after all cost well over a hundred kronor. Maybe Gösta had hoped for whisky. Mike had considered it, but felt uncertain about giving spirits as it wasn't Christmas.

Pah. He pushed the thought to one side. It had nothing to do with not being pleased. The reason that Gösta had seemed somewhat reserved was that he preferred to keep a distance, socially, given that Mike was still his patient.

That's all it was. Nothing more.

The day that Mike finished his treatment, they could go out for dinner, the four of them.

Gösta's wife seemed nice. She and Nour would definitely get on. Who wouldn't get on with Nour? Mike got butter-flies even thinking about her. It almost made him giggle.

And like a sign from God, she came through the door. Sanna rushed out into the hall to greet her. Mike stood back, embarrassed by his childish joy. It couldn't get any better. He waited his turn and kissed her on the mouth. He took her coat and hung it up on a hook.

'Smells good,' she said.

'Mince sauce,' Mike said. 'Red.'

Nour didn't get it.

'Difficult to explain. It's very sophisticated.'

Sanna disappeared into the sitting room, where Mike was less than delighted to discover that she had emptied her vast collection of Lego on to the fluffy carpet. No matter how much he hoovered and beat that carpet, Mike knew that there would always be pieces left in it somewhere.

He poured a glass of red wine and handed it to Nour.

'Thank you,' she said, taking the glass.

Mike looked at her and smiled.

Nour didn't know why.

'I just feel so happy,' he said.

51

Gösta took his time, went through his entire repertoire. Ylva's moaning and writhing verged on the limits of credible, but Gösta had no objections. Afterwards, he lay beside her for a long while, breathing heavily, his chest sweaty.

'You certainly can do this,' he said.

'Thank you.'

'Are you happy?'

'I'm happy,' Ylva said.

'Mike and Sanna are happy too,' Gösta said.

Ylva didn't answer. Neither he nor Marianne ever mentioned her family by accident, there was always a reason.

'He's together with Nour now, as you know. I've never seen him happier. Sanna, too, for that matter. No one is indispensable, least of all you.'

Ylva said nothing.

'It would certainly cause a scene if you were to ring on the doorbell now.'

'I'm happy here,' Ylva said.

'You are? Yes, you've got it good, considering why you're here.'

'With you,' Ylva said. 'I'm happy with you.'

Gösta laughed, sat up on the edge of the bed and started to pull on his underpants.

'Marianne says that I've had my fun.'

'Is she jealous?'

Gösta stared at her. She lowered her eyes.

'I'm sorry.'

'We are not a couple, you and I. You're just a cheap whore and you should be grateful that I come here and fuck you at all. I do it out of kindness, do you understand?'

'I know, thank you. I'm sorry.'

'Your thousand and one nights are coming to an end, it's all getting about routine. No matter how I twist and turn you, you still only have three holes. I'll be back tomorrow.

And I want to be surprised. Do you understand? If you don't manage that, then we'll have to think of something.'

Just as Ylva thought, Mike's spontaneous visit and bottle of wine had made Gösta and Marianne nervous. It was an intrusion into their private life, a sign that the outside world was moving in, that the trap was set. And so they had to get rid of Ylva. She had become a burden. Without her, they had nothing to hide; without her, they could open their home and welcome people in.

Marianne wanted Ylva to do it herself. As atonement. Gösta did too. That was their original plan.

They both underlined the desperateness of her situation. That even if she stayed alive, there was no future. She was a whore and could never be anything else.

And of course they were right. Everyone would ask the same question: why didn't you escape? Why didn't you even try?

But Ylva hadn't thought of giving them the satisfaction of committing suicide. She would never be able to do it. She hoped that they would kill her when she was asleep. Or that they'd poison her so she lost consciousness. Though she did want to know what they would do with her afterwards. She wanted to be buried. To give Mike and Sanna something definite, to release them so they could carry on with their lives.

She wished that she didn't know what was coming. But it was too obvious. Gösta was going to fuck her one last time. She could do her best, in the hope of a few days' respite. But there was no point. Next time, he'd have to take her as the dead sex doll he'd forced her to become.

Right now she just needed to sleep. She was tired and wanted to enjoy dreams that didn't tie her down. When she woke up, she would remember them.

Ylva crept under the covers, stretched her hand out to the floor lamp and flicked the switch.

Everything went dark.

52

When the phone call came, Calle Collin wasn't surprised; he'd been waiting for it.

The managing editor of *Family Journal* said hello, asked how things were and what the weather was like in the capital. Time-wasting pleasantries that people from outside Stockholm persisted in using.

Get to the point, Calle thought, put me out of my misery.

'So,' the managing editor said.

Finally.

'I saw the editor-in-chief and we discussed a few things and we both agree. Very strongly, in fact.'

Not another round. Why couldn't they just tell him to get lost and leave it at that?

'And . . .' the managing editor continued.

Here it comes. Calle closed his eyes and held his breath. At best, he would be allowed to do humiliating celebrity questionnaires on holiday weekends. *Who will you be kissing at Easter? How we celebrate Christmas* and *My favourite drinking song*. Sitting on the phone for hours in pursuit of has-been TV celebrities who wanted to show their sad faces again.

'Yes?' Calle tried.

'We don't want any suicide,' the managing editor said. 'I know that *The Friends' Post* doesn't write about suicide for the simple reason that it can be contagious. Our readership is older and hopefully more sensible, but all the same. We don't write about suicide because it's just too awful. There's nothing redeeming about suicide and we are thankfully not in the single copy market. So we don't write about it. Full stop.'

'N-no suicide?' Calle stuttered.

Had Ylva's husband not spoken to her? Were they still interested? Did they still want his series about people who had died too young?

'Why?' the managing editor asked. 'Do you not agree?'

'Yes,' Calle said. 'Absolutely. I wouldn't even dream of writing about suicide. Never.'

'Good, I'm so glad. In that case, all I have to say is good luck. How soon do you think we can have the first article?'

When Calle got off the phone, he was so happy that he turned up the volume on the stereo and danced around his flat, until he realised that someone in the building opposite was staring at him.

Blackness and silence, like floating in the universe. Ylva could almost see our blue planet in the distance; from a distance where nothing on the face of the Earth mattered. All worldly struggles became as dust. Her journey would soon be over, the ephemeral will-o'-the-wisp that was Ylva would go out. It was no big deal, it happened every second, every day, and had done since the beginning of time.

Her life had taken some sharp turns. Her difficult childhood that degenerated and ended in catastrophe. It had all started as a game, but then had serious consequences. The shrink's crazy daughter. Annika.

The long interlude when she imagined that this was how life was meant to be. The summers on the boat, Mike, happiness with Sanna.

337

The distractions that Ylva had amused herself with once she grew weary of all that.

Sanna could manage fine without her mother, Ylva knew that, even if the knowledge hurt. Her memory of Ylva had probably already faded. She could hear Mike's voice, how he would try to remind her.

You remember Mummy?

A misguided concern for Ylva's memory that would only result in bad conscience, and for Sanna, the vague feeling of a person who had once existed but was no longer there.

Ylva tried to imagine the world through her daughter's eyes. What would Sanna remember about her? It could be anything. A time when Ylva had been a bit boisterous, tickled her on the tummy, had a pillow fight. Or perhaps a comment, hopefully something kind. Maybe a film they had seen together. Definitely one of their many swims in the sea. Ylva jumping into the water, of course. The other mothers used the steps, some of them even lowered themselves into the water. How cautious could you be! Women under forty who reversed into the water up to their waist and then fell back, splashing around like old women and stretching their legs. Without getting their hair wet.

Ylva decided that that would be her gift to the world,

that that was how she would live on. As the mother who jumped into the water from the jetty and only used the steps to get out. Ylva was happy. It wasn't a bad legacy to leave behind.

She didn't want to dwell on the last chapter of her life. It was what it was and it would soon be over. Even if she chose to see it from their perspective, she had atoned for her crime and was reconciled with the thought that every person had the capacity for good and evil inside them.

She stretched out her hand, pressed the light switch and suddenly the room was bathed in light from the floor lamp. She went to the toilet for a pee, flushed, and then crept back under the covers. She stretched out her hand, pressed the light switch, darkness.

She pressed the light switch again, light.

And again, darkness.

Naturally.

Yes, naturally.

53

Jörgen Petersson had found a real dive.

'Three for a hundred kronor,' said the quarter billionaire, blithely, as he put six beers down on the table in front of him.

He slid three of them over to Calle.

'Couldn't we have started with one each?' Calle asked.

'Don't worry – my treat,' Jörgen assured him.

'Great.'

'Just saves us getting up and down, you know how it is. So, tell me about your progress.'

Calle told him about the telephone call with the managing editor, how he had ducked and held the receiver out from his ear fearing that his eardrum would be damaged by the bollocking she was going to give him. And how it had all turned out so well in the end.

'So one doesn't write about suicide, does one not?' Jörgen mocked.

'No,' Calle said. 'Because there's always some dimwit who reads it and is inspired: *I want to be in the papers too.*'

'*Even if it's the last thing I do,*' Jörgen quipped.

'Exactly. Strange that the managing editor felt that she had to point it out. A bit of a let-down, I must say.'

'And, ta-da, you've transformed progress into a setback,' Jörgen said. 'You're about as pessimistic as Krösamaja in the Emil books. We could put you in a room full of stockbrokers and as soon as the stock market rose, you'd put your hands to your head and say: "First they'll go blue in the face and then they'll die."'

'And it wouldn't be a moment too soon,' Calle said.

'I couldn't agree with you more. Cheers.'

'Cheers.'

They finished their first beers, pushed the empty glasses to one side and grabbed another full one. Nursing it like a baby bottle.

'So suicide is contagious?' Jörgen said thoughtfully.

341

'Just like seasickness,' said Calle.

'Do you remember that girl at school who took her own life?'

'Who?'

'Annika, the shrink's daughter.'

'Oh yes, her.'

'Lived in the white pile down by the water,' Jörgen prompted. 'Right out on the point. Black dog that ran up and down the fence barking whenever you cycled past.'

'Oh, her. Hanged herself, didn't she?'

'Think so. No one really went into any details. Good-looking mum, as far as I can remember.'

'Not my department,' Calle sniffed.

'The dad wasn't bad, either. Richard Gere type.'

'Now you're talking.'

'The daughter, on the other hand, was rather plain,' Jörgen added, philosophically.

'God, listen to yourself.'

'It's possible she might've grown out of it, who knows? But I don't think she'd ever be as sexy as her mum. Don't you remember her? She was the neighbourhood MILF. Used to rake the gravel on the driveway.'

Calle started, diving into his own thoughts: rake the gravel.

The elderly woman in Hittarp. The one who looked familiar. Who had pointed out where Michael Zetterberg lived.

'That dog used to make a racket, with all the boys cycling past for an ogle,' Jörgen said.

She had been raking the gravel. Just like she always had. It was her, Annika's mum.

Jörgen snapped his fingers under his friend's nose.

'Calle? Hello? Can you hear me?'

The flex was attached to the base of the floor lamp. About two hundred centimetres from the switch, which was one of those you can tap with your foot. But Ylva normally turned off the light with her hand, so she didn't need to get out of bed. There was about one and a half metres of cord from the switch to the wall, which had been pushed under the bed so it wouldn't look messy.

When the switch was off, there was no power supply to the lamp.

Gösta and Marianne had overwhelmed her and locked her up with the help of a stun gun. Now it was Ylva's turn to give them a taste of their own medicine.

She was not a whore, she was the mother who jumped into the water.

Ylva got out of bed and went over to the kitchen area. It was pitch-black, but she knew every centimetre of her limited space. She took the scissors and knife and went back to bed. The light was off, so no electricity could run past the switch.

She crouched down, felt around for the flex and cut it as close to the base as she could. Using the knife, she stripped the ends, bent the wires out so there was a couple of centimetres between them. She stuck the end of the flex back under the base.

From now on, she wouldn't turn the light on, under any circumstances. Not until the time was right.

She went back to the kitchen area and returned the scissors and knife to their place on the counter, where they were visible, in accordance with the rules. She was punished harshly if she ever broke or forgot the rules.

She opened the drawer and took out the fork, the only piece of metal cutlery she had been given to eat with, went back to the bed and hid it under the mattress.

She was going to give him a new experience, a completely new experience.

'No,' Calle Collin said. 'No, no, don't.'

They had drunk six beers each and the bill was now

standing at four hundred kronor. Plus twenty for a bowl of peanuts. Calle couldn't imagine that his super wealthy friend would leave anything more than ten as a tip.

'It can't just be a coincidence,' Jörgen said.

'Pff, well,' Calle started. 'What's the connection, you reckon?'

'I don't bloody know. But one thing's for sure, I don't believe in coincidences.'

'You don't need to believe in coincidences,' Calle said. 'In our middle-class world – and I hope you don't mind me including you in it, you just happen to have earned a lot more – but our middle-class world is so laughably small that it doesn't take much. Do you know what I do when I'm feeling a bit paranoid and want to stoke the flames? I look up old adversaries on Facebook. All the bastards are there. You get a picture of the person in question and can see all the idiot's friends. Then you look at the updates and discover a whole new raft of friends. And I tell you, you don't have to do that many times before you come across a name that you know from somewhere else. You press on that and, hey presto, a new person and a new gallery of friends. Updates, and a click on. The whole world is con-nected. The fact that Annika's parents live where they live, among other well-to-do folk, is not a coincidence. They always flock together. So they can avoid people with different points of view. So much for coincidence, thank you very much.'

'God, you're drunk,' Jörgen stated.

'I'm not drunk.'

'Okay, well, think about this then. Imagine if the shrink and his MILF wife for some reason held the Gang of Four responsible for Annika's death ...'

'There is no Gang of Four. They were friends for a while in secondary school, and, yes, they were bullies and should have all been locked away, I couldn't agree more, but, and I mean a big but, they weren't a gang. After Class Nine you never saw them together at all. One of the guys dropped out of school, if I remember right. Jörgen, you bloody weirdo moneybags, are you listening to me?'

'I'm listening, I'm listening.'

'Well, look like it then, don't just sit there staring at the wall.'

'I'm not staring at the wall, I'm thinking.'

'Would it be possible to share some of your great thoughts?'

'I think I'm right. The group split after Annika's suicide.

I don't give a damn what you say, I think I'm going to call Ylva's husband.'

'Then I won't have a job to speak of.'

'I can employ you, you can write my memoirs.'

'That wouldn't be very difficult: woke up, won the lottery, fell asleep.'

'I'm going to phone him,' Jörgen said.

'You're not,' Calle retorted.

'Just try stopping me.'

'Jörgen, for fuck's sake, come on. I'll lose my job, I will, I'm not joking.'

54

'Karlsson speaking.'

The chief inspector answered without his eyes leaving the page. The local newspaper was a must for a man in his position.

'Yes, hello, my name is Jörgen Petersson.'

Stockholmer, Karlsson thought to himself.

'I'm trying to get hold of whoever is dealing with the disappearance of Ylva Zetterberg,' Jörgen continued. 'She went missing about a year and a half ago, if I've understood correctly.'

The missing away-player, Karlsson thought, who was

killed by her jealous husband, the one with the crocodile tears. Who's still a free man. Without a body, they couldn't link him to the murder.

'That'll be me,' Karlsson said.

'I've got some information that I think might be of interest.'

'Let's hear it then,' Karlsson said, and returned to his reading.

Anyone who had information that was of interest had to be pumped for it; anyone who had information that was of interest didn't say, *I've got some information that might be of interest.* That was a given, just like anyone who said they had a good sense of humour or claimed they were intelligent usually didn't or wasn't.

'Right,' Jörgen started. 'I went to school with Ylva. Brevik School on Lidingö, here in Stockholm.'

'Okay.'

I'm from Liiiiiidingö, so what I'm saying is important, Karlsson mimicked to himself, and turned the page of his newspaper. He noticed that Kallbadhuset would be opening again soon. About bloody time. How long does it take to renovate a swimming pool?

'Ylva was part of a gang. There was her and three guys. Real tough nuts. We called them the Gang of Four.'

'Goodness.'

'I know it sounds stupid, but please hear me out.'

'I'm listening.'

'The guys are all dead,' Jörgen said.

Karlsson studied the cinema listings. He'd got it into his head that a film he wanted to see was showing, but none of the titles rang any bells. He'd just have to rent a DVD as usual.

'That's not good,' he said.

'No,' Jörgen said, 'and now Ylva's missing as well. It seems like too much of a coincidence.'

'Mm.'

Karlsson had got to the TV page. He skimmed over it. Nothing that was very exciting.

'It can't just be coincidence,' Jörgen insisted.

'These tough guys,' Karlsson said. 'How did they die?'

'One died from cancer about three years ago. Another was murdered and the third was killed in a motorbike accident in Africa about a year ago.'

'Doesn't sound good,' Karlsson said. 'But I don't quite see the connection. Other than that they were friends when they were younger.'

'Well,' Jörgen said, 'there was a girl.'

'Ylva?'

'No, another one.'

'I see.'

A complete tosser here, Karlsson thought to himself.

'Annika Lundin,' Jorgen told him.

'Annika, right.'

'And she committed suicide.'

Karlsson tutted and folded his newspaper. He leaned back in his chair and looked out the window.

'After that, the Gang of Four all went their own ways.'

'After what?'

'After she committed suicide. Aren't you listening?'

'I'm listening.'

'Good. Because what's really interesting is that Annika's parents, Gösta and Marianne Lundin, moved to a house opposite Ylva.'

'Gösta and Marianne . . .?'

'Lundin,' Jörgen repeated. 'I don't think it's a coincidence.'

'No, that doesn't sound likely.' Karlsson yawned.

'You should talk to them,' Jörgen said.

'Absolutely,' Karlsson replied. 'Do you have a number I can reach you on?'

Jörgen gave him his mobile number and his home numbers. Karlsson pretended to write them down.

'I'll be in touch as soon as I know anything more,' Karlsson assured him. 'Thank you for calling.'

He replaced the receiver. Cinema, he thought. What was that film I wanted to see?

Gerda knocked gingerly on the door and interrupted his musing.

'Lunch?' his colleague asked.

Karlsson got up and put on his jacket.

'Not a bad idea.'

Jörgen Petersson knew how far-fetched it all sounded. In his mind it was absolutely crystal clear, it was only when he put it into words that it sounded crazy. The chief inspector had promised to talk to the Lundins, but Jörgen doubted he would even pick up the phone.

He wondered if the policeman would have treated him differently if he'd known who he was and what he represented. The answer was without a doubt yes. But he couldn't exactly fax over a copy of his bank balance. Did he know anyone who could pitch his case? Anyone in the police? Nope. The closest thing to a legal acquaintance he could think of was the commercial lawyer he used to write contracts.

If Calle Collin's Facebook theory was true, and these lawyers knew other perverters of the law, who in turn were mates with the public prosecutor, who hung out with the police, he might just get through after sitting on the phone for a few hours. And any credibility he had would by then be jaded, as his conspiracy had been passed from one person to the next like Chinese whispers.

If Jörgen Petersson wanted to get any further, he had to talk directly to Ylva's husband. No matter that he'd promised Calle he wouldn't. Ylva's husband was the only one who might listen.

It was possible that Jörgen was barking up the wrong tree, that his thoughts were as mad as they sounded, but there remained one question that had to be answered. And that question could only be put directly to Ylva's husband.

55

Ylva looked at the screen. She saw Mike and Nour and Sanna get in the car. Sanna was in the back seat again, but seemed happy with her lot. Their routine seemed as pain-free as a morning routine could be with a daughter who took an eternity to spread the butter, ate slower than a snail and wasn't happy until her laces were done up in a perfect bow and both ends were the same length.

This was possibly the last time she would see them. Certainly the last time she would see them on the screen. She wasn't sad. It was fine now. More than enough.

She turned off the screen, lay down on the bed and

closed her eyes. She went through the plan again. If it was actually a plan; she wasn't sure. She intended to do what she'd decided, then what would be would be, she had no control over the result.

The glass of water, the flex, the fork under the mattress.

She had never hit anyone, didn't know what to do. She took out the fork and felt the points. It wasn't particularly sharp. She pulled back the sheet and stabbed the mattress. It didn't even make a hole.

The eyes, she thought, she had to get his eyes.

She replaced the fork under the mattress, tucked in the sheet and went into the bathroom and looked at herself in the mirror. She was someone else now, not the same person who had been dragged down into the cellar eighteen months ago. She wondered whether Mike would recognise her.

Ylva went back out to the kitchen, looked in the fridge. She had to eat something and rest.

No matter what happened, this would be her last day in captivity.

Mike leaned towards Nour and kissed her on the mouth.

'See you this evening.'

'Yes. Bye.'

Nour jumped out, closed the car door and waved again from the pavement. Mike slipped into gear and drove off, watching in the rear-view mirror as Nour disappeared into the office.

He felt warm and happy inside.

The euphoria stayed with him until lunch. And was then replaced by melancholy.

Nothing in particular had drowned out the rush. No bad news, unfavourable forecasts or complaining employees to dampen his joy. His mood hadn't been caused by a sudden drop in his blood sugar levels, troublesome flashbacks or a difficult task. It was just a normal mood swing and Mike welcomed the change. If he went around in the euphoric state he'd been in all morning, he'd soon make himself unpopular. Either that or he'd be forced to move to Norway, where that kind of hearty behaviour was not seen as suspect.

He opened a new report and started to read. Three-quarters of an hour later he put down the tome, rubbed the base of his nose under his glasses and realised that he was none the wiser. It was just another of those long-winded volumes that managed to say nothing while costing the company a small fortune, their only merit being that they provided cowardly middle managers with something to blame when things went wrong.

Mike looked at the clock and saw that he could go home with a clear conscience. He called Nour from the car, but she still had some unfinished business at work, so she'd get the bus.

'See you later then,' he said. 'I'll make supper.'

Mike went to the supermarket and wandered aimlessly around looking for inspiration. Meat, hmm. Fish, nah. Chicken, not again. Vegetarian, was there anything other than broccoli quiche?

Gösta was also in the supermarket and they exchanged a few words about how difficult it was to get variety.

It was going to have to be spaghetti with blue cheese sauce and fried bacon. And a salad. Mike picked out what he needed and added a few things for breakfast.

He drove over to the school and went into the after-school club. He couldn't see Sanna and the staff looked at him in surprise. His heart started to pound and for a fraction of a second Mike was launched into an abyss, until he remembered that Sanna had started music lessons. He smiled and walked towards a door, through which out-of-tune music could be heard.

He knocked gently on the door and went in.

Three . . . blind . . . mice. La-la-la. See . . . how . . .

Mike didn't need to book Berwaldhallen concert hall quite yet.

'Bravo.' He applauded. 'Sounds good.'

'I can do it better,' Sanna told him.

'I thought it sounded great. Are you done?'

He looked at the music teacher, who nodded gallantly.

'Well, then we'll say thank you and goodbye.'

'Thank you,' Sanna said.

'You're welcome,' the teacher replied. 'See you next week.'

Sanna bounded out of the room and ran towards the car.

'Can I sit in the front?'

'Sweetie, it's only a couple of hundred metres. It's not worth moving the booster.'

'Okay.'

What? Mike thought. No protest? Sanna got into the back without any grumbles and carried on playing her recorder. He wanted to say something encouraging. He just didn't know what.

'Is it fun, playing the recorder?'

358

'Yes,' she said breathlessly and carried on blowing.
Three . . . blind . . . mice.

Ylva was made up, dressed and ready. Hair in a ponytail. Gösta liked to pull it when he came. A kind of show of animal ecstasy.

She looked the way he wanted her to look. But this time she hadn't used any lubricant. He wasn't going to penetrate her, not today, not ever again.

Hearing his knock, she took a deep breath and checked that everything was in place. The glass of water next to the wall.

She stood in her designated spot, put her hands on her head, pulled back her elbows to push out her chest, and pouted.

He opened the door. He was holding a bottle of champagne and two glasses.

He looked automatically to the right, to check that the knife, scissors, kettle and iron were visible on the worktop, that she had no weapons and wouldn't try anything stupid.

'Thought we could celebrate,' he said, and held up the bottle.

Ylva went down on her knees, hands behind her back.

She had planned it all, practised it again and again. She daren't risk deviating from the plan.

He put the bottle down by the sink, locked the door and looked at her.

'Can't you wait?'

Ylva shook her head slowly, still with her eyes lowered and mouth open.

'Well, you'll have to restrain yourself,' he said, and pulled the golden foil from the top of the bottle and started to unwind the metal thread.

Ylva stayed on her knees, watched him pull out the cork with a bang and fill the glasses.

He came over to her, looked down.

'You're a horny little bitch, aren't you? Here.'

He held out a glass.

'You've earned it,' he said.

Ylva took the glass and filled her mouth, without swallowing. She put the glass down beside her on the floor and started to unbutton his trousers. She put his cock in her mouth, let the bubbles tickle his glans and the champagne spill slowly down his balls.

She filled her mouth with what was left in the glass and pulled his chinos down. He let her because he didn't want to get them wet. He stepped out of his trousers and underpants and even let her take off his socks.

She put the clothes in a pile on the bed and took him in her mouth again. The bubbles ran out of her mouth and down the inside of his thigh as she eagerly held up her glass for more, without taking him out of her mouth. He filled the glass, and then continued to pour directly from the bottle, over her face and the base of his cock.

The floor was starting to get wet and Gösta was standing in a puddle. Ylva's plan was working. Champagne was as good as water. The important thing was that it was wet.

Ylva looked up at him and saw that he was looking at her as if she was a whore he had paid for and could do what he liked with. It was an expression she knew only too well and it was always a precursor to sexual violence.

Ylva filled her mouth again. She put down the glass and clasped her hands behind her back. He grabbed hold of her ponytail and pushed himself in even further. Ylva felt a gagging reflex but pretended to be loving it.

She had the flex in her hands behind her back. As soon as he let go of the ponytail, as soon as he let go . . .

56

The ringing of the phone was a welcome distraction. The off-key notes of the recorder were playing on a loop in the sitting room and Mike didn't have the heart to tell his daughter to stop.

The display read *unknown number*. Mike assumed it was Nour, ringing from work. He closed the door to the sitting room and picked it up.

'Hi,' he said in a soft voice.

'Er, hello,' said the surprised voice on the other end. 'My name is Jörgen Petersson. I'd like to speak to Michael Zetterberg.'

'Speaking,' said Mike, with more authority.

'Am I calling at a bad time?'

'No, no, not at all, but I don't buy things over the phone.'

'That's not why I'm calling,' Jörgen said.

Mike felt his stomach knot in an instant.

'I want you to listen,' Jörgen told him, 'and please don't hang up until you've heard what I have to say.'

Mike sank down on a chair.

'What do you want?' he asked.

'I went to Brevik School with your wife,' Jörgen explained.

'My wife is missing,' Mike said in a sharp voice. 'Why won't you leave me alone?'

'Just one question,' Jörgen continued. 'What has Ylva said about Gösta and Marianne Lundin?'

Mike didn't understand.

'Gösta and Marianne Lundin had a daughter, who also went to school with us,' Petersson continued. 'She committed suicide. The guys that Ylva went around with at school are all dead. I think there's a connection. I think your wife, in some way, had something to do with Annika's suicide – that is, I think Gösta and Marianne Lundin hold her responsible for Annika's death. Michael, are you there? Michael . . .?'

Gösta let go of her ponytail. Ylva pulled back her head and slipped the flex from behind. She put the stripped wires on his shiny cock and flicked the switch.

A flame flared, there was a muffled pop and everything went dark.

Ylva didn't know what she'd expected, but it certainly wasn't that the fuse would blow.

'Jesus fucking damn bugger shit!'

His voice was fraught with pain and Ylva heard him sink to the floor with his back against the wall. He was breathing in great gasps and she could smell burned flesh.

'I'm going to fucking kill you, you fucking whore.'

She fumbled under the mattress for the fork, grabbed it and started to stab at his face. The first time he managed to stop her, the second time the fork sunk into the cartilage of his cheek.

Ylva leapt up on to the bed, pulled his trousers over and dug into the pockets for the keys.

'I'm not a whore,' she screamed, kicking her leg into the black air where she guessed he was slumped. 'I'm the mother who jumps into the water. Do you hear me, you perverted bastard? I'm the mother who jumps into the water.'

She found the keys and ran to the door. Her hands were shaking and she couldn't get the key in the lock. She heard him heave himself to his feet with great effort. She wasn't going to manage in time.

'I'm going to wring your neck, d'you hear?'

He struggled slowly towards her. The knife and scissors were on the worktop. She hesitated. Door or knife?

She took two steps over to the kitchenette, grabbed the knife and held it out in front of her in the dark. The keys in her right hand, the knife in the left. It felt wrong. The knife should be in the right hand. She had no strength or coordination in her left hand.

She could hear his breathing, his rattling laugh. There was no chance she'd make it to the door. He was on his feet and he was stronger.

'Getting closer,' he said. 'This will end how it always ends. You can't hide.'

She stood by the worktop, trying to breathe silently. He was only a couple of metres away. He was standing still, now, listening, just like her.

'Are you hiding in the kitchen? That's not a good place

to hide. The kitchen's narrow and pokey, there's barely any room there at all.'

He took two steps towards her.

'Have I fucked you in the kitchen? I think I'll do that – fuck you in the kitchen. I'm going to fuck you in the kitchen with a broken bottle, d'you hear?'

A couple of metres separated them. She waited, held her breath. She had to change hands, get the knife in her right hand. But it was impossible to do it without making a noise and giving away where she was. She'd only have one chance, and it was important that the knife went in deep so he couldn't come after her.

She crouched down. Her joints creaked faintly.

'Well, well, well. Old creaky knees, eh? So you're in the kitchen, just as I thought. Waiting for me to come and get you. To fuck you just the way you like it.'

He shuffled nearer. She felt his presence up close. Something swept over her head and the champagne bottle smashed against the wall behind her.

She threw the keys over towards the door to make a distracting noise, switched the knife to her right hand and propelled herself up. The knife sunk into his torso. She pulled it out and stabbed again.

'All the way in,' she screamed. 'How does that feel? All the way in.'

She pushed the knife in a third time and left it there. He collapsed on the floor.

Ylva was on her feet, staggering to the door, feeling around on the floor, finding the keys. Her hands were steady. She put the key in the lock and turned it.

57

Mike felt feverish and sick. Too many thoughts that refused to stay still. Too fast for him to grasp, not waiting to be understood – taunting him like a circle of school children. No matter how Mike twisted and turned, the theories and questions were there, ready to push him back into the ring.

Another nutter, had to be. In cahoots with that reporter from the weeklies who had accosted him in his own home the week before. Some sicko who got pleasure from spreading shit, just to be in the momentous presence of death for a short while. Death was attractive, no doubt about it. It drew nutters like honey. Like the ones who phoned people who'd lost someone in the tsunami and claimed that their loved one was alive and would be home soon.

And yet ... Gösta had had a daughter. She had died young. He didn't want to talk about it. Which was perfectly understandable. Especially given Gösta and Mike's respective roles.

What has Ylva said about Gösta and Marianne Lundin?

What did he mean? Why link Ylva with Gösta and Marianne? They weren't even living here when she disappeared, they moved in just afterwards. Or about the same time. At the same time.

But whenever it was, Ylva had never mentioned meeting the new neighbours who'd just moved in.

And why would the crackpot want to drag Gösta and Marianne Lundin into this? How did he even know who they were?

Mike didn't get it. Then it hit him.

A patient.

Naturally. The guy who'd called him was one of Gösta's patients. Who'd somehow heard Mike and Gösta talking and in his sick mind had created a parallel world.

That had to be it. There was no other explanation.

Mike let out a deep sigh. He was still upset, almost

369

shaking. He blinked his hot eyes furiously. But the relief spread through his body like a Friday drink.

Slowly he started to register the world around him, let himself be filled with visual impressions and sounds. Which were coming from a recorder in the sitting room.

Three blind mice, three blind mice . . . la-la-la . . . see how they run.

The recorder's equivalent to 'Für Elise' on the piano.

The recorder's equivalent to 'Smoke on the Water' on . . .

Mike remembered the first time he'd met Gösta, when they realised that they were neighbours. Gösta had moved into the house in Sundsliden, where they had done out the cellar and spent a lot of money on a music studio. Gösta had played on an air guitar while he hummed a riff from Deep Purple's 'Smoke on the Water'.

He was obviously being ironic, but *that* ironic?

Thoughts started to chafe again. Mike found it hard to swallow.

He had told Gösta about the idiot from the magazine who had gone on about the three dead guys. Gösta had said that he didn't quite follow. *Three dead*, he'd said. *That's not much to talk about. Three people who'd gone to the same school together who'd died young.*

Three . . .

But there weren't three: with Ylva there were four. Mike and Gösta always talked about Ylva as if she was dead. Neither of them thought she would come back. But Gösta didn't say four, he said three.

Probably just a mistake, but still.

Mike shook off the uncomfortable thought, turned on the water, let it run cold, then drank straight from the tap.

Anyway, it would be easy enough to check.

He opened the door to the sitting room.

'Hey, sweetie, you're playing really well. Do you know what I think?'

She shook her head.

'I think we should go over to Gösta and Marianne, you know, the ones who live in the white house on Sundsliden. He's got a music studio there. Maybe we could record you playing. Then you can listen to it later and see how much you've learned. Would you like that?'

Ylva turned the key and opened the first door. It was so easy, she couldn't understand why she hadn't done it before. She picked out the next key and felt something cold against her back. She felt it again.

Ylva gasped for breath, but her lungs were only half full. She breathed out and there was blood in her mouth. One of her lungs had been punctured. To her surprise, she thought of it as a burst balloon. She hadn't thought about her lungs as balloons. Lungs were pieces of meat, squishy and revolting, like most things inside the body, not balloons.

She turned the key and pushed open door number two. A faint light slipped down the stairs and into the cellar. Gösta was lying on the floor behind her, unable to get up again. The fork was still in his cheek, just below the eye. The kitchen knife was in his hand.

Ylva was surprised that his hate was so intense that he had managed to pull the knife out of his own body, stand up and stab her in the back twice. It didn't worry her, she was neither frightened nor angry, but it did fill her with surprise.

'We were children,' she said, her mouth full of blood. 'Children.'

She staggered towards the stairs. The blood ran from her mouth, down her chin, past the black bra, down her stomach, knickers and thighs. She grabbed hold of the banister, used all her strength to haul herself up the stairs, step by step.

She heard voices, felt the cool air full of fantastic smells.

She wanted to fill her lungs, both lungs, but immediately started to cough. The light got brighter. Real daylight, blinding light from the sun.

Only a few steps more.

58

Mike held his daughter's hand.

'Are we in a hurry?' Sanna asked.

'No, no. We're not in a hurry. Just thought we'd do it before we eat. Nour will be back soon. Would be a nice surprise for her, wouldn't it? Her own disc.'

'What's that?'

'A sound recording. And you can play it again and again. Whenever you want.'

'Like on the computer.'

'Exactly.'

They cut across the grass, which was wet. Mike held the gate open for Sanna, saw Marianne in the kitchen window and raised his hand in greeting. She opened the door before they'd even got there.

'Gösta's not at home,' she said.

'Oh, that's a pity,' Mike said, and placed his hands on his daughter's shoulders. 'Sanna's just started to play the recorder. I thought I'd ask if we could borrow the studio to record her first attempts.'

'The studio?' Marianne didn't understand.

'The music studio,' Mike said. 'In the cellar.'

'Oh, right. No, I'm afraid that's not possible.'

Mike smiled, taken aback. Marianne shifted her weight.

'Gösta's very particular about his studio. He doesn't like to let anyone in. It's his space for him.'

'I understand, I understand.'

Mike started to feel uncertain, didn't know how to approach it.

'Okay,' he said, and smiled because he couldn't think of anything else. 'Thanks anyway.'

He hoped that it didn't sound ironic.

'It's not that he means any harm,' Marianne said.

'No, no, I understand. Tell him I was asking for him.'

'I will do.'

Mike turned around as if to go, then changed his mind at the last moment.

'Your daughter,' he said.

The reaction was immediate. Mike could see it in her eyes. But it was so unthinkable that he carried on talking, even though in that instant he had understood.

'She went to school with Ylva,' he said, and felt all the pieces falling into place.

Everything the nutter had ranted about was right, every single word was true.

Marianne said nothing. The woman's face was cold and guarded, revealing no emotion.

There was a noise from the cellar.

'I'm going down into the cellar,' Mike said, and stepped past Marianne.

At that moment Sanna screamed when she saw a bloody, deathly white and nearly naked person appear at the top of the stairs.

Mike stopped in his tracks. The woman's skin looked plastic, almost see-through. The only thing that looked real was the blood that was running from her mouth down her body. She raised her arm, stretched it out. Mike knew the whole time who she was, but it was only in the way that she lifted her arm that he recognised his wife.

59

Mike rushed to Ylva, put her arm round his shoulder and supported her out of the house. They stopped at the gate. She couldn't go any further. Mike sat down on the gravel, rested Ylva's head in his lap, rocked her. Sanna stood at a distance, not daring to go forward.

'I'm sorry,' Ylva said.

Mike shook his head.

'Forgive me,' he said.

Ylva looked around for her daughter.

'Sanna,' Mike called. 'It's Mummy.'

He held out his hand, urged her to come over. She

hesitated. The bloody woman frightened her. The red teeth, the grey hair, the porcelain-white skin. She wanted to run away, not to see.

Ylva lifted her hand slightly.

Sanna went over, hunkered down.

'I can play,' she said. 'Do you want to hear?'

There was blood everywhere and, to begin with, the ambulance crew couldn't work out who was actually injured. When Mike told them that the blood on his clothes was from Ylva, they quickly examined her, lifted her on to a stretcher and carried her towards the ambulance. A group of hypnotised, staring neighbours moved out of the way so they could pass.

Mike took Sanna by the hand and followed them to the ambulance. The paramedic put an oxygen mask on Ylva's face and the driver got in behind the wheel.

Ylva had lost consciousness to the sound of 'Three Blind Mice'. Mike thought he had seen something like a smile on her lips.

Loud voices could be heard from outside. Through the ambulance window, Mike saw flames in Gösta and Marianne's kitchen. The curtain caught fire, flames licked the ceiling.

'Is there anyone in the house?' the ambulance driver asked.

Mike didn't answer. He watched the paramedic pressing a rubber pump that was attached to the mask on Ylva's face, and he knew that they were helping her breathe. He knew that they were in an ambulance that was now accelerating up the hill, he was aware that he was holding his daughter's hand. And yet it all washed over him.

The paramedic repeated the driver's question: 'Is there anyone in the house?'

'Yes,' Sanna replied.

The ambulance driver radioed the emergency switchboard. The paramedic was working frenetically. Administering oxygen, injecting fluid, saying things. Everything was happening like it was all a film.

Mike thought it was a strange job, working so close to death. Unnecessarily dramatic, he thought. The paramedic talked constantly, informing the driver of the patient's condition. Eventually he looked at his watch. He said the time clearly and loudly. Mike couldn't understand what difference it made.

Ylva was going to be dead for a long time.

60

Someone took Mike's bloody clothes and gave him a short-sleeved white cotton shirt with the county council logo printed on the front. They were shown to a waiting room. Sanna sat on her father's knee, Nour in the chair beside them. All three holding hands, saying nothing.

The waiting room had a lino floor and blond-wood furniture with green covers.

Sanna leaned forward and picked up a comic from the table. She gave it to Mike. He read for her.

About Bamse and Lille Skutt and some idiot who gets into a fight but is forgiven in the end and allowed back into the fold. Mike carried on reading the next story, even though he wasn't sure whether Sanna was actually listening or just wanted to hear his voice. She bounced her foot up and down in the air, nervously.

The door opened and they all looked up at the nurse.

'She's ready now,' she said.

They walked down the corridor. The nurse stopped in front of a door and turned to make sure they were prepared.

Nour looked at Mike.

'I don't know if . . .'

'Yes,' Mike said, and pressed her hand. 'Please.'

The nurse opened the door and let them through.

Ylva was lying on the bed with a blanket pulled up to her shoulders. Her head was resting peacefully on the pillow. Her eyes were closed and the blood had been washed away. The pale, almost porcelain skin was less alarming in the dimmed light. It was so obvious that it was a body, not a person.

Nour stayed back, let Mike and Sanna go and sit on the chairs by the bed.

After a few minutes, Mike's back started to heave and he

fell forward over his dead wife. Sanna reached out her hand and comforted him.

When they finally got up, their eyes were red and swollen.

Nour held out her arms and embraced them both.

61

Karlsson tasted the coffee and returned to the article he had just read. There were a lot of facts to take in and memorise. Some of the information was new to him, and friends and acquaintances would press him for bonus material as if he was a DVD.

And he had to feed the mob or he would lose face. *Not informed? Not up-to-date? You should know, you work for the police. Didn't you head the investigation?*

Gerda was sitting opposite with his own copy of the newspaper. He too was reading the article, for the same reason.

'Jesus, what sick bastards.'

'Tell me about it.'

'How long was she down there?'

'Over a year and a half.'

'And her husband was being treated by the guy all that time? You'd think he might have guessed.'

'Yeah.'

'Strange that he didn't suspect.'

'Who? The man?'

'Yes.'

'Very strange.'

'Completely improbable.'

'We couldn't have done anything.'

'What could we have done? How could you guess this?'

Gerda carried on reading the article.

'Was he already dead?'

'The man? Must have been. No smoke in his lungs. Unlike the old bird who set fire to the place.'

'So Ylva snuffed him?'

'Yep.'

'Good job.'

'Really.'

'But strange that she didn't do it earlier.'

'She probably didn't have the chance.'

'No. But all the same.'

Karlsson shook his head.

'Fucking pervert.'

Gerda agreed. Someone knocked on the door. They both looked up. A colleague was standing there holding a newspaper open with a grin on his face.

'Have you seen this?'

He threw the paper on the desk and went away whistling. Gerda rounded the desk so he could read at the same time as Karlsson.

Ylva died unnecessarily – police ignored important tips.

The article included a picture of Karlsson and described the phone call that he'd taken a few days earlier.

'Who's written this crap?' Karlsson said, and looked for the byline. 'Calle Collin? Who the fuck is Calle Collin?'

62

Sanna had managed to nag her dad into an extra swim. She wanted to swim in the swell of the six-thirty ferry to Oslo. The ferry left Copenhagen at five and sailed past Hittarp at twenty past six. The swell reached the shore ten minutes later. The waves weren't that big, but they were reliable and on time.

Mike hadn't been hard to convince. He believed that nagging should pay off. What other possibilities did children have to influence things? Besides, he had swum in the half-six waves himself as a child, and it was a tradition that he wanted to pass on.

They got there in good time, and Sanna jumped into the water immediately. She didn't want to wait around on the jetty. It was the water she wanted, the waves were a bonus. Nour sat on the bench.

'Here they come,' Mike said, and pointed out into the sound.

Sanna swam quickly over to the ladder and climbed up. She stood ready and looked at her father.

'Aren't you going to swim?'

'Of course,' he said, and pulled at the drawstring of his trunks.

'Are you ready?'

'Yes.'

'Let's see a proper dive then,' Nour called.

Sanna stood with her eyes fixed on the waves that were slowly coming closer. She patted her father on the stomach.

'The biggest one, okay?'

'Of course.'

'Now.'

They ran to the edge of the jetty and jumped in.

63

Annika is so happy that she's been asked, that they even know who she is. The gang who sits perched on the windowsill, leaning against the glass, looking down on everyone. Places where the ones who ruled always sat and where the losers and the oppressed didn't dare go. They know who she is because Ylva shouted after her and walked with her to the gymnasium and even invited her to her house. It's not going to be a party or anything, they're just going to hang out. TV? No TV. Fuck TV. No, no.

But what's strange is that they've got nothing to talk about, and Ylva hardly says anything, not until the boys come with the alcohol that they've smuggled out of their parents' bar cabinets, and then she talks non-stop, and they drink and get all weird and laugh and Annika tries to laugh as well, but when they ask her why she's laughing she has no explanation and Ylva says she thinks Annika should show her tits to the boys, Annika doesn't understand why and Ylva asks if she doesn't dare, if she thinks that the boys haven't seen tits before, and the boys think that Annika should show them her tits as well and Annika thinks that maybe she should get up and go, but they're just joking with her, can't she take a joke, and they fill her glass and now she's part of it all again and they laugh together and then Ylva says that she thinks Annika should definitely show her tits, come on, just a flash, and everyone looks at her, it's easy enough, just a quick flash and Annika lifts her top and then pulls it down again, but I didn't get to see, says one of the boys, we didn't either, shout the other two, and they nag at her again and Ylva says that it doesn't really matter now, she's already shown them, let them have a look, and Annika lifts her top and holds it up and one of the boys wants to touch them, just to feel, but Annika doesn't want him to, oh don't be so boring, and Annika lets the boy touch her and then the other two want to touch her too and they say that she's got nice tits and they feel good and Annika takes her top off completely and kisses one of the boys and they all laugh and drink more and Annika wants to put her top on again, but Ylva thinks she should take off her trousers instead and show her fanny, but Annika doesn't want to show her fanny, come on why not, what does it matter, but Annika still doesn't want to, Ylva says she's being ridiculous, as if there's anything wrong with showing your fanny, but do as you please, Annika, and the boys laugh and Ylva says that it was worse to show your breasts really as your fanny is just a triangle of hair and she and the boys have already been in a sauna together and stayed with each other and seen everything there is to see and there's nothing weird about it, no, the boys say, then you can start, Annika says, but they think it's a better idea for Annika to do it as she's already taken some of her clothes off and she just needs to show it and once again all their attention is focused on Annika and there are friendly smiles and encouraging nods and it's not weird at all, and okay, she undoes the button and they applaud, and it's quite fun and she pulls down the zip and sways her naked chest seductively and the boys clap and Ylva thinks she's fun and Annika pulls her trousers about halfway down her thigh, puts her thumbs inside the top of her knickers, rolls them down, lets them get a glimpse of her hair and they shriek, more more, and Annika pulls down her knickers and shows them it all, and her success is complete and maybe Annika will regret it later but the moment in itself is great and beautiful and something she will remember and carry around inside and she pulls up her knickers again and they boo her, but she sits back down on the sofa, gets hold of her jeans and lifts her bum to pull them on properly, but then one of the boys holds them down and they laugh and joke and Annika tells him to let go, but he just jokes and one of the boys says that she's beautiful and has an amazing body and he kisses her for real and caresses her breasts and she feels the others pulling off her jeans, but she can't bear to protest and she still has her knickers on and it's nice and uncomfortable at the same time and the boy who's kissing her lets his hand wander down and he puts it over her knickers and the hand feels warm and nice and she thinks that maybe this is what it's like because she doesn't know anything else and she hears someone undoing their trousers but it's not the boy she's kissing and she stops kissing and looks in surprise at Ylva and the boy who now has his trousers and boxers round his ankles and who shuffles over and Annika isn't kissing anyone any more and she doesn't want to, but no one listens and everything is quiet and there's no laughing and the boy pushes himself in and comes quickly and the next boy is waiting and Ylva is sitting beside them watching, and the third boy penetrates her and complains that he's last because now she's been widened and it's like putting your cock in a bucket of warm water and they laugh and then there's nothing more to do so they pull up their trousers, button them up and drink what's left in their glasses and Annika sits rolled up like a ball as she tries to pull on her clothes, piece by piece, and Ylva says that it's maybe best if she goes and if she says anything they'll say what a fucking whore she is, fucking three guys like that on the same night.

NOV   2012